"Maybe you could tell me about it some other time." The band finished a song. There were a few hoots and a smattering of applause. A slow tune started up. "Could we dance instead?" Brooke asked it straightforwardly, without a hint of coyness.

"Dance?"

"You don't want to?"

"Oh, no. I mean, yes, I'd love to dance. Sure."

"Okay."

Sean's hands slid over her bare shoulders. He pulled her close and they moved very slowly.

"Are you cold?" he whispered.

She didn't answer, merely shook her head no.

They continued to dance, barely moving until the song ended. It was only then that Sean noticed with a smile she was still wearing just one shoe.

Billy Joe York

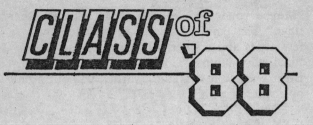

by Linda A. Cooney

Freshman
Sophomore
Junior
Senior

CLASS of '88

JUNIOR

Linda A. Cooney

SCHOLASTIC INC.
New York Toronto London Auckland Sydney

ISBN 0-590-40350-8

12 11 10 9 8 7 6 5 4   8 9/8 0 1 2/9

Printed in the U.S.A.   01

First Scholastic printing, October 1987

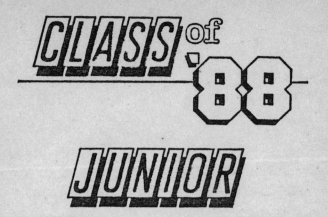

CLASS of '88

JUNIOR

CHAPTER 1

Allie didn't want her plane to land. She wrapped her arms around her chest, made tight fists with her hands, and closed her eyes. If only there was a way to stay in the air forever — in that nowhere, nothing, nonplace between where she was going and where she had been.

"Allie." Her father tapped her impatiently. "ALLIE."

Allie moved her head ever so slightly. He had that look again, the one he had so often lately — the look that said, You're a jerk, Allie, a pain; you're driving the entire family crazy. Why, WHY, couldn't they just leave her alone?

"Is your seat belt fastened?" he asked, irritated. He was cleaning his glasses on the corner of his sweater, and his eyes looked puffy and tired. "The pilot turned on the sign."

"I know." Allie buckled her belt, making a big deal out of pulling it tightly for her father's benefit. He put his glasses back on and huffed loudly. He huffed at her a lot these days.

The sparkly blue of the San Francisco Bay was getting closer as was the Golden Gate Bridge and the geometric jumble that was downtown. For six months Allie had waited to see this sight — dreamed about it, ached for it. Now all she felt was emptiness and dread. The airplane sailed down gracefully, but the closer they got to the runway, the more Allie's stomach began to dip and dive. When they landed with a soft bounce, tears suddenly exploded down her cheeks. That was another thing that happened a lot lately — she would start crying anytime, anywhere, without warning. Allie pushed the tears away with the heel of her hand and faced the glass, avoiding her father and her mother, who sat one row ahead with her brother and baby sister, Emily.

Why was she crying this time? Because she wanted to go back to New York City? NO! Because she was so happy to be home? Oh, no. Because she wished with all her heart that she could be somewhere and someone else entirely? One more tear slipped down. Maybe.

"Al, honey." Her mother was turned around in her seat, stretching back. Allie rubbed her eyes as if she had an itch and looked sullenly up at her. "Meg, Celia, Nick, and Sean are meeting you. I know how you've missed them."

Dread turned to hot, shaky panic. Meg and Celia, Sean and Nick! Allie'd assumed she wouldn't have to see her old friends for at least a day or two. Who told them to come and meet her? Why did they think she'd want to see them?

Tears were pressing so hard that Allie had to swallow and clench them back.

Her mother and father exchanged glances, then her mother stuck her arm back and patted Allie's knee. "It was supposed to be a surprise, but I thought you might want some warning so you could freshen up."

"Freshen up?" Allie threw back sarcastically. What was that supposed to mean? Take five minutes and transform herself back into the person she was last September? Put on pink lipstick and brush her hair out of her face and pretend her parents hadn't dragged her across the country just so her father could guest-teach two quarters at Columbia? Too bad they hadn't stopped to worry last fall how much Allie might miss her old friends and everything else about junior year in Redwood Hills. "I look fine."

"All right." Mrs. Simon paused as if she was trying not to lose her temper. "I know they all missed you."

Allie's stomach took another nose dive. The terminal was getting closer, and she tried to make out figures inside. Were Celia and Meg really in there — or Sean or Nick? Why would they be there, anyway? Sure, the five of them had been inseparable since they were little. Sure, her friends had written every other week — sent collective letters from all four of them with Meg's school report, Celia's gossip, Sean's computer drawings, and Nick's jokes. But Allie hadn't written back for the last two months. One of them must have figured out that something had changed.

Allie slumped in her seat and chewed her fingers as the plane taxied closer. The only comforting thing she could think of was that at least L.P., her ex-boyfriend, wouldn't be there, too. She was sure he wouldn't have made the trek to greet her. He probably wouldn't go two feet out of his way to see her ever again.

Her mother was still watching her.

"What?" Allie demanded.

"It'll be nice to see all your old classmates again on Monday, don't you think?"

"Oh, boy. I can't wait."

Mrs. Simon gave a disgusted huff of her own, then turned back to take care of Emily.

Allie was praying that everyone would just leave her alone, when the pilot's voice came over the loudspeaker. He was telling the passengers there was going to be a short delay before deplaning and would people please sit back down and refasten their seat belts. Everyone groaned. Everyone except Allie. She wanted to stay right there forever.

At that same moment Meg McCall was tearing through the airline terminal, her long dark hair flying, a rolled-up banner tucked against her chest like a football. "Hurry up, you guys, we're late!"

"Yeah. Let's go!" Nick called to Celia and Sean.

A few yards back, Celia, Nick's cousin, was daintily holding up the hem of her narrow skirt, her legs flinging out on either side as if they were on hinges. "Wait up! I can't run in this."

4

Sean brought up the rear. He was balancing six or seven small packages in his long arms and pitched one up to Meg as she climbed onto the escalator. "McCall, take this!"

Meg tried to catch it, but her arms were full with her banner. She giggled, "I can't," and batted it down to Nick with her elbow.

Nick caught it, examined the sack, wiped his forehead with the cuff of his letterman's jacket, and hollered down to Sean, "Pendleton, why didn't you leave all this stuff in your van?"

"The back door doesn't lock," Sean yelled back up, ducking to avoid a man with a suitcase on his shoulder. "Somebody could've stolen it."

Nick held up his free hand and Sean tossed up another sack. "Who would want to steal a thousand-year-old egg?"

"Hey." Sean wrinkled up his freckled face. "Robin Chin in my physics class told me it's a great delicacy."

"Yuuuuuck," Meg and Nick moaned at the same time.

Sean laughed. "You guys have no sense of adventure."

Meg got to the top first, leaped off the escalator, and stared up at a video screen that showed the gate numbers of the incoming flights. "This way," she told the others, pointing down the crowded corridor. She took off.

The others hurried up the escalator and followed. It was hard to tell who was the most excited to see Allie again — Meg, who'd painted an elaborate Welcome Home banner; Celia, who'd dressed up as if she was on her first date;

5

Nick, who couldn't slow to a walk; or Sean, who'd insisted they stop in San Francisco and pick up a feast for the ride home, including sour dough bread, cheese, Ghiradelli chocolate, and from Chinatown, something called a thousand-year-old egg.

Celia and Sean scrambled until they caught up with Meg and Nick. They marched four abreast.

"What if we miss her plane?" Meg worried.

"Does she know we're coming?" Nick asked.

"No," Celia said, looking for the gate and combing her blonde hair with her fingers. "But her parents do. Meg's dad told my mom, who told your mom, who told Mrs. Simon not to tell Allie so it'd be a surprise."

Sean scratched his head. "That's clear."

They walked even faster when they spotted Allie's arrival gate. Nick led the way now. He was jogging and looking back, as if he was waiting to receive a pass. When he reached the gate, he stopped and caught his breath. About thirty people were already waiting, staring expectantly at the empty doorway.

"Somebody help me with this," Meg said as she knelt down and unrolled her banner. Celia and Nick held down the other end, while Sean watched the door and guarded his delicacies.

"Maybe we shouldn't have surprised her," Nick said, still panting and whipping off his jacket. "She might start screaming or something. You know how Allie gets."

Sean laughed. "Remember that time when we

were about twelve and we went to see that Bill Murray movie and Allie laughed so hard?"

"Yeah," Nick nodded. "With that goofy laugh of hers."

"Instead of laughing at the movie, everybody laughed at her laughing." Sean did an affectionate imitation of Allie's laugh, which was somewhere between a gurgle and a moose call. They all cracked up.

Meg interrupted them before they lifted her banner. She stared at it. "Okay. What do you guys think? I know I'm not the greatest artist, but. . . ."

The banner said WE MISSED YOU! and had a caricature of Allie — her wispy brown hair in a corkscrew perm — wearing a wild hot pink and purple outfit with tons of jewelry and a cocked hat. She was grinning and sticking out her tongue.

"It's great."

"It's perfect."

"That's Allie."

Celia grabbed the other end from Nick and the two girls lifted it, letting it wave slightly as they stood on tiptoes, so eager to see Allie again. Passengers were starting to struggle off the plane, and just next to Celia an older man and woman rushed into each other's arms for the first reunion.

"When's the last time you talked to her?" Meg asked Celia softly, so the guys wouldn't hear.

Celia was jumping and craning her neck. "Christmas. My mother won't let me call very often. She's allergic to phone bills."

Meg smiled. "I called a few weeks ago, but

Al wasn't home. I just wondered what happened with her and L.P. — why they broke up."

"You know how long-distance relationships are."

"Yeah." Meg switched banner hands, putting the tired one in her jeans pocket. People were pouring out of the plane now. There was an Indian man wearing a turban, a bunch of college students, and about twenty old people who looked as if they were part of a tour. No Allie yet. "I wondered why she stopped writing — you know, if that meant anything."

Celia shook her head. "Nah. Allie's always been a terrible letter writer. She probably figured she'd be home soon, so why bother."

Both girls watched the passengers again.

"There's Mrs. Simon and Emily!" shouted Sean, jumping up and waving his loaf of bread. "Look how big Emily is." Mrs. Simon smiled and came over, hugging each of them.

"I'm so glad you came," Mrs. Simon told them, her eyes teary. "Allie will be out soon." Just then Emily wiggled out of her arms and started running. Mrs. Simon took off to catch her.

"Mr. Simon!" yelled Nick, spotting Allie's father, who was yawning and stretching his arms. He was with Fletcher, Allie's brother. He waved, but gestured that he was heading over to help his wife, who was still chasing Emily down the corridor.

The four friends continued to stare into the crowd, searching for Allie.

"Where is she!" Celia demanded.

"I don't see her."

"Me, either."

Celia squinted and squirmed, bobbing around bodies and trying to see every person who came through the door. She was just about to tell the tall man in front of her that he was blocking her view, when a pale round face, no more than a foot away, came into focus.

"Allie?"

There was silence, even in the crazy airport there was total and complete silence.

"Allie, is that you?"

Two more steps and Celia was closer, her eyes wide open.

"Oh, my God."

Celia gasped and brought a hand to her mouth. Her side of the banner fell to the floor with a loud *clack*. She didn't pick it up. Instead she blinked, and blinked again, sure that the person standing right in front of her couldn't really be her childhood best friend. That was when she realized that Allie'd been standing right next to her for quite some time. "Allie?"

"Hi," Allie said, her mouth unsmiling, her eyes glued to the floor.

Celia stared. Allie wore a dark, shapeless dress. Her lips were coated with pasty white lipstick. Her hair hung limply to her shoulders and was dyed a flat, unnatural black. Three earrings were looped through one ear and she wore a jacket that said NO FUTURE.

"Allie?" Celia repeated, her voice barely coming out of her throat.

Meg's face was taut with shock, and Nick was looking around the terminal as if they'd made a mistake.

Sean took a step back. "Is that Allie?" he whispered.

Meg scooped up her banner, hiding it in her arms. "Yes."

They all stood frozen while the gushy reunions continued around them. Allie stared off at the newspaper dispensers. Unable to stand the silence any longer, she started to leave.

With a bold move, Nick stopped her. He flung his arm around her shoulder, but she was as stiff as a dead tree. "Hey, Al, great new hairdo," he teased, bumping her with his hip.

Allie shrugged. "Yeah."

While the other three still gawked, unbelieving, Nick wound his arms around Allie's small frame, picked her up, and swung her. She was so light that she flew like a little kid, her black-booted feet flailing. When he put her down there was a hint of color in her face, but still she didn't smile.

"We all missed you, Al," Nick told her.

They all watched her as Allie slowly lifted her head. Her eyes were filled with tears that quickly overflowed and ran down her face faster than she could brush them away. Meg, Celia, and Sean rushed in to hug her.

For a moment the five of them stood in a tight huddle. Out of the corner of her eye Celia saw Allie's parents, waiting by a long ramp with Fletcher and Emily. They looked tired and worried. Celia didn't have to guess why.

Allie suddenly broke away from her friends and, almost running, passed her parents, and headed down the ramp. She stopped briefly to call back in a flat voice, "Thanks for meeting me. You don't have to wait for the bags. I'll go home with my folks."

Then the crowd swallowed her up and she was gone.

The four friends stared down the ramp for a long time. People rushed around them. A man plowed into Sean with a huge suitcase. Three laughing stewardesses almost tripped over Meg. But the four of them did not move.

"Should we go after her?" Meg asked finally.

"I think we should. Come on," Celia insisted.

Nobody led the way.

Nick stuck his hands in his pockets. "She obviously didn't want to drive home with us."

"She sure didn't," Sean said definitely. He faced the other direction. "Let's go."

They marched quietly out of the terminal, blinking when they made it out to the parking lot. After the long, rainy winter it was finally sunny and bright, but no one smiled or remarked about the great weather as they crossed the asphalt and climbed into Sean's parents' van.

The ride from San Francisco back to Redwood Hills took almost two hours. They were all the way to Vacaville and not one of them had spoken a word. Sean was drumming on the steering wheel and humming with the radio, Nick was chewing on sour dough bread, and Meg was staring out the window.

Celia had a stack of photos on her lap. They

were all of things that Allie had missed by being away most of her junior year. There was a picture of Nick and his latest girl friend, a senior named Darcy; lots of photos of Meg being crowned a junior homecoming princess; a shot of Celia organizing the fall fashion show; Celia's boyfriend Tim Holt in front of his family's new house in Marin; finally there was a close-up of Sean accepting the junior science achievement award.

Now Celia had the feeling Allie wouldn't be very interested in what a successful junior year the rest of them were having. She tossed the photos in the back and sat up. "WHAT HAP-PENED?" she cried out in her most worried voice.

The van skitted into the next lane. "Cici, don't scare me like that," Sean fired back.

Celia pounded the seat and shouted, "What happened to ALLIE?!"

Nobody could answer.

"She looks so awful," Celia moaned.

"Maybe that's how they dress in New York," offered Meg. "Allie always liked to look differ-ent."

"Meg," Celia insisted, "this is beyond different. She can't walk around school like that. Besides, you don't start looking that way unless you want everyone to think you're totally out there."

"Maybe she does," offered Sean.

"Sean!" Celia huffed.

"All I know," Nick added, "is that she sure doesn't seem very happy."

"Well, I'm not giving up on her," Celia said,

tossing back her blonde hair and sitting tall. "She was my best friend for ten years and as far as I'm concerned, she's still my best friend. She needs me now, and I'm going to be there. I'm going to do everything I can to make her like the rest of us again."

Sean turned back, crossed his eyes, and stuck out his tongue. "She may not want to be like me."

"Sean, this isn't funny," Celia snapped. "We're juniors. Pretty soon we'll be applying to college and getting jobs. We don't have time to waste looking and acting like weirdos."

Sean made one more face, but when Celia frowned, he nodded and started drumming the steering wheel again. "You're right," he said finally. "Boy, are you right."

CHAPTER 2

"Celia, this is dumb!"

"I know what I'm doing, Meg."

"Then why did you drag her to this meeting? It's her first day back. You have to give her time to get used to school again."

"Let me handle this, Meg. I know Allie best."

"We have to wait until Allie is ready to talk to us. Then, when we know what happened in New York, we can figure out what to do."

"Meg, it's better to throw her into everything we can at school. Otherwise she'll just sit by herself and mope. Believe me, I know!"

"You do not!"

Meg clamped a hand over her mouth, as she realized that other kids could hear her. She and Celia were wedged between the world globe and a bust of Lincoln in the corner of Lyons' history room. It was lunchtime, and juniors were rush-

14

ing in to attend their first class-planning meeting after spring break.

"Look at her!" Meg whispered as Allie walked into the room. "She looks miserable." Celia turned to stare at their friend, who had found her way to the very last chair at the end of the room. Today Allie wore black jeans and heavy boots that looked like leftovers from the Marine Corps. Her hair flopped over her face, which she rested on her desktop.

Immediately Meg and Celia shifted, staring instead at Mr. Lyons' datelines, the dusty blackboard erasers, and the sun gleaming on the quad through the side windows. "She does look awful," Celia whispered. "Everybody's talking about her clothes already."

"That's not what I mean," Meg shot back. That was another thing they'd argued about. Celia wanted to change Allie's clothes and hair as soon as possible, but Meg — who almost always wore Levi's, blazers, and running shoes — didn't think that was so important.

Just then Patrick Delancie, the class president, came into the room. Meg waved to him. "We've got to get this meeting started," Meg told Celia. "We'll talk about Allie later." She gestured for Celia to sit in the desk next to Allie and made her way up to the front.

"Meg! There you are!" Patrick said, rushing up to greet Meg with a huge smile. He flicked his long, wavy hair away from his face and stuck his hands in the pocket of his down vest, which had a tiny SAVE THE WHALES pin on the lapel. "I looked for you after third period, but I guess you went a different way."

"Yeah, I did." Meg nodded. She and Celia had met Allie between every class, no matter how out of the way it was.

"It seems like so long since I've seen you," Patrick said in a soft, sweet voice. He crossed his long legs, and stared down at his cowboy boots. "How was vacation?"

Meg craned her neck to check as Celia slid in beside Allie. She and Celia exchanged frustrated looks. Allie still looked as if she was stuck in detention instead of a class meeting.

"Meg?" Patrick said again. He nudged her shoulder.

"Huh? Oh." Meg shook her head. "Sorry. My vacation was only fair. How about yours?"

"Good. I spent most of the week stuffing envelopes at the 'Save Portola Creek' office. Yours was only fair, though?" He waited eagerly for Meg to say something else. When she didn't, he smiled and shrugged. "Well, I guess we'd better start."

"Okay."

Patrick stood up. "Um, could everybody quiet down so we can get going?" He waved his arms, but his voice was so gentle that the ruckus completely drowned him out. "We have to finish the plans for College Day, and that's pretty important," he continued wishfully.

Meg usually let Patrick struggle to get her classmates' attention, but today she was not in a patient mood. Besides, she could tell that people really had spring fever. Sam Pond and his pals from the swim team were tossing around Sean's bicycle helmet; Nick had come into the room only to start tickling his new girl friend, Darcy; and Sarah Hammond and her crew of jabbermouths sounded like the spring birds. There was was only one thing to do. Meg hopped on the table, put her pinkies in her mouth, and whistled as loudly as she could. The blast made even her own head ring, but at least Darcy stopped giggling.

"HEY," Meg yelled, "I know it's major spring fever time. But if we get started right away we can get out of here in time to still get some sun." Meg was answered by a few catcalls and footstomps. Greg Kendall winked and pitched a ball of tin foil at her. She tossed it back, and it landed right in his open lunch sack.

"Thanks, Meg," Patrick whispered as he stepped forward. "Okay, everybody. Welcome back. The main thing we have to do today is finish planning our College Day. Most of the colleges we contacted are sending at least one representative who can tell us whatever we need to know about that school. We have room for twenty tables in the cafeteria, and so far we have sixteen colleges definitely coming." He handed Meg a stack of papers to pass out. "Here's a list so you can see who they are."

Meg hopped down. As she passed out the sheets, she snuck back to check on Allie. The ruckus bubbled up again. Nick was teasing Sam Pond and the other swimmers about having shaved their heads to increase their speed, and Darcy was instructing a bunch of girls on how to write a college application essay.

17

Meg crept back to Allie's desk. "Hi, Al," she whispered.

Allie lifted one hand and then slapped it down on the desktop. Meg could see the stripe of light brown roots at the top of her crown. Her fingers were all bitten and red and she wore about ten silver rings that looked more like washers or tool parts than jewelry. When Meg handed Allie a list, Allie pushed it back without looking at it.

Once more Meg tried to force the list on Allie, but Allie wasn't interested. She was wearing that jacket, the one that said NO FUTURE. It was an ordinary guy's jacket, almost like the ones the school bus drivers wore . . . but those words! Meg had just started thinking about what college she would go to, what she wanted to do and be. Wasn't that what junior year was about? How could a junior even conceive of an idea like there not being a future?

Thinking about it made a scary knot in Meg's stomach. As she walked up to rejoin Patrick, she wondered if forcing Allie to attend this meeting that was all about THE FUTURE wasn't the worst thing they could possibly do. By the time she made it back up front, she'd decided. It was much too soon to throw Allie into this. The only thing to do was get this meeting over as quickly as possible, so with a nod from Patrick, Meg took the floor.

"Okay, guys," Meg called out. "For College Day, we still have to address invitation letters to all the parents and get volunteers to set up tables. I'll put info and sign-up lists on Mrs. Weaver's door, so everybody check those. Also, remember we're sponsoring the dance this Friday, so tell all your friends to come. I think that's it. Do you want to add anything, Patrick?"

Patrick looked a little stunned. Why was she suddenly acting like the tardy bell had just gone off? But before he could say anything, Darcy Kiltner was on her feet. "Wait a minute," Darcy objected, waving her paper and raking back her glossy chestnut hair with an open hand. "There's something wrong here."

"Is there?" Meg could feel her teeth clench and her eyes narrow. She usually succeeded in hiding the fact that Darcy drove her completely up the wall, but she was too edgy today for that kind of control. "And what's that, Darcy?"

Darcy stood confidently, her riding boots planted, her hands on her hips, showing off a curvy figure under a pair of jodhpurs and a ruffly high-necked blouse. "Why isn't Bradley College on this list?"

"Darcy, you're a senior. This is the junior College Day. Why do you care?"

"Meg, you're lucky that a senior comes to your meetings to share her experience and knowledge with you."

In front of everyone, they glared at each other. Meg noticed that Allie had propped her chin on her fist to watch. At least something had finally sparked her interest.

Meg knew she shouldn't react this way to Darcy. She'd told herself over and over: Darcy was just another in the long line of pretty, popular, irritating girls that Nick had dated this year. Darcy's bossiness was particularly hard to take, as were her dimples and her phony *National Velvet* wardrobe — Darcy had never been on a horse in her life. Of course, Meg had considered the fact that Darcy drove her nuts because of her own feelings for Nick. There was a time when Meg was in love with Nick, and she sometimes thought there'd been times when he felt the same way about her. But that was over. They were too mature for that now. They were just old, close friends.

"Darcy," Meg answered, "we decided that it was more important to invite California colleges and bigger schools first. Bradley is out of state and expensive. With only twenty tables, we didn't think we should invite a school that only one or two kids might be interested in."

"Meg, I think more than one or two kids are interested, and it's silly not to invite them," Darcy shot back. "Bradley is one of the best schools in the country. I'm going there. Just because Bradley is special is no reason to pass it over."

Meg resisted tossing back that the only thing special about Bradley was that it had a reputation for being one of the biggest party schools in the country . . . but just barely. Fortunately, Patrick had taken the floor. "Actually, Darcy," he said calmly, "with midterms coming up, we don't have time to arrange for another school. But if you think it's so important to have Bradley come to our College Day, why don't you take care of inviting them yourself. We'll save them a table."

Darcy glanced around the room, all the junior

eyes on her. Lastly she looked at Nick and melted into a smile. "All right," she said soothingly, "I will." She sat back down next to Nick.

"Okay," Meg finished. "Check Weaver's board. And everybody make sure and come to our dance Friday. Meeting's over!"

Everybody gathered books, Greg Kendall and John Purdy made Meg promise to dance with them on Friday, then kids jostled and pushed through the door. Even Patrick, who was gathering all the empty lunch sacks the others had left behind, rushed out.

Meg was about to follow her classmates, when she saw that Allie still sat with her head on the desk. Celia was next to her and Sean was hanging around, too, trying to balance his milk carton on top of the globe. When Nick came back in from the hall — without Darcy — Meg decided to stay.

Nick pulled the door shut and it suddenly felt very private. Just the five of them. "How's it going, Al?" Nick asked gently. Compared to Allie's pallor, his golden hair and flushed cheeks looked even healthier than usual. "Almost fifth period and you're still alive," he added as a little joke.

"That's only because she didn't eat in the cafeteria," Sean cracked.

One corner of Allie's white-lipsticked mouth lifted — a little.

Celia leaned forward. "Allie, I know this is hard for you, but you have to do this stuff. We'll all be with you every step of the way, and I promise it'll get easier. Now, there's the dance on Friday night. What else?" Celia looked to her friends for support.

Nick knew what his cousin was hinting at and hesitated. Finally he tousled Allie's hair and smiled. "We have this ridiculous bowling contest going on. Meg and I are the two team captains so you can imagine how inept it is. If you come, I promise to trick Meg and get you on my team."

"I'll need you more on my team, Al," Meg encouraged. "Last time I bowled a ten."

Nick got up and pulled Sean over, turning him around so Allie could read the back of Sean's shirt. "You can wear Sean's lucky bowling shirt. He'll loan it to you." The shirt said *Bowl at Jarvis Lanes. It's a ball!* Sean rearranged his shirt and went back over to the globe.

When Allie put her head back down, Nick stepped in and touched the top of his head to hers. Then he shook his head as if they were two puppies, or bear cubs. "And all the juniors have to go on this field trip to see some Shakespeare play in San Francisco next week. You always liked that kind of stuff. If you don't sit with me on the bus and explain it all, I'll never understand what's going on."

Allie finally raised her head. Her face looked softer, younger. More like the old Allie. But her round, dark eyes were still watery and sad. "You guys really want me to do all this stuff with you?"

Celia nodded.

"You're crazy."

"You just figured that out?" Nick teased.

"We always were," Meg added, trying to keep

things light. "That's why the five of us stuck together."

"Yeah, Al," said Celia. "Some things just don't change. We can't break up a good fivesome now."

Sean, who hadn't said much the whole lunch period, gave the globe a spin.

Allie dragged herself to her feet, as if the whole thing was too painful to think about. "I guess I could give it a try. Maybe it'll be okay."

They all smiled and nodded. But nobody was really sure.

CHAPTER 3

By the middle of the dance on Friday night, it was Sean's turn to take care of Allie. Meg was manning the door. Darcy was hanging all over Nick. Celia's boyfriend, Tim, was down from Marin. So Sean had been assigned Allie-duty. He felt as if he was baby-sitting.

"What do you think of the band?" he projected over the music. The juniors had hired The Crashers, a local rock group who wore leopard leotards and eye makeup.

"They're okay," Allie answered without enthusiasm.

Sean didn't think too much of the band, either, but he'd thought Allie might find some kind of kinship with them. She was dressed in a huge black sweater, those Marine Corps boots, a long, baggy black skirt, her NO FUTURE jacket, and a black bowler hat.

"Patrick was right," Sean said, trying to make

conversation. "We should have hired The Carports."

They stood next to the cafeteria stage, so close to the band's speakers that Sean's limbs vibrated. Crepe paper streamers floated from the ceiling like seaweed upside down. The band lights waved back and forth. Sean tried to concentrate on the decorations and the music. Anything was better than paying attention to all the stares and whispers that were going on around them.

"You want to dance?" he asked Allie. The last thing he wanted to do was dance, but he'd promised Meg and Celia that he'd ask.

Allie raised her face to the ceiling and gave one silent laugh, almost as if someone had slapped her on the back. "No way."

"That's okay." Sean tried not to show his relief. He wouldn't have admitted it to his friends, but he wasn't crazy about being Allie's guardian this evening. He thought he'd be happier than any of them to have Allie home again. But now he found himself secretly wishing that this strange, unhappy creature wasn't really a close friend. The idea that people might think Allie was his date for this dance made him feel creepy-crawly inside.

They continued to bob to the beat, as if they were enthralled with the music, when there was suddenly a crackle like fried rice. A tiny puff of smoke coughed out of one of the PA speakers and The Crashers stopped playing. At first Sean was glad for the break — they were in the midst of a truly brutal rendition of a Van Halen song. Then he heard three voices behind him screaming too intently to realize that the music had stopped.

"SHE'S A HEAVY METAL CHIC."

"NO, SHE'S A BURNOUT."

"LET'S FACE IT, SHE'S JUST A CREEP," they all blurted at the same time.

Sean whipped around just as Eve Brandsteen, Marilyn Cooper, and Greg Kendall realized that they were yelling their heads off in a perfectly quiet cafeteria. They looked at Sean, mortified. Finally a few giggles eased the tension and the band began hitting random notes on the synthesizer, checking the problem with their busted speaker.

There was no way Allie couldn't have heard them. She turned even paler and her face lost any hint of liveliness. She folded down on the back corner of the band platform, reached in her pocket, and put on a pair of dark glasses.

What was Sean supposed to do? He'd been hearing the names all week. Not just burnout and creep, but punker, new wavo, fieldie, headbanger . . . names he didn't even understand. But what the names stood for didn't matter. They were just like the names he used to be called: nerd, brain, weirdo, geek. As far as he was concerned, they all meant the same thing.

Sean walked over and patted Allie's shoulder. He was glad they were in the dark, that the only light passing over them was the occasional wave of blue. He wasn't sure exactly why, but for him this year the names had almost stopped. Maybe it was because he'd finally put on some muscle by biking up Capitola Mountain and guzzling

26

protein malts. Maybe his classmates had matured enough to appreciate things like winning a science contest. Maybe it was just because he changed the style of his shirts. Whatever, all Sean knew was that he never wanted to go back to that name category again.

Sean was about to sit down next to Allie, when a raspy voice from the band platform stopped him.

"Hey, you, uh . . . dude," the musician said to Sean.

The guitar player climbed down off the stage, not looking at Allie. Even the guys in the band didn't want to deal with her.

"Hey, man," the guitarist continued. "If I give you some tools, can you take a look at that speaker? We can use a backup while you work on it."

Sean had helped the band set up and talked electronics with them. He'd attended a special workshop at Redwood college sophomore year and built his own preamp over the summer. Not only did he like working on audio equipment, but the idea of getting away from the dance floor really appealed to him.

But he knew he wasn't supposed to leave Allie alone. Celia wasn't in sight — she was probably outside necking with Tim before he had to begin his long drive home. Meg was still at the front desk, surrounded by Patrick Delancie and some other guys, and Nick was tickling Darcy.

"Al, I have to go in the kitchen and take a look at this speaker. Is that okay?"

Allie didn't look up. "Of course."

Sean put the speaker and a metal tool box on an audiovisual cart. "Stay right here." He pointed to the platform and felt ridiculous. It was like telling a puppy to wait for you outside the supermarket.

Sean rolled the cart away as the band hooked up their backup speaker and started to play again. He looked back once to check on Allie. She was still on the edge of the platform with her legs outstretched, her arms folded, her sunglasses half covering her face. Quickly, Sean wheeled the cart into the kitchen, but before he could close the door, Sam Pond and two other swimmers appeared in the doorway.

"What's going on, Dr. Science?" Sam asked.

Since Sean had won the award that fall, the jocks called him Dr. Science. It was still a name, but at least a name that was tinged with respect.

"Speaker's busted," Sean answered.

"You gonna fix it?" asked Gary Schilling, swim team captain.

"I'm gonna try, man."

The swimmers gathered around as Sean unscrewed the back of the speaker and pried it open. As they moved in around him Sean felt his shoulders rise and his stomach clench. He had no reason to get nervous; it was some leftover instinct that was no longer necessary. Sean didn't have to go back generations to find the reason for this fear. It was within his three years at Redwood High that jocks like Sam and Gary had bullied and humiliated him. He tried his best to appear cool, even a little tough.

"Whoa," marveled Sam, rubbing his shaved

head and staring at the mess of wires. "You really understand what's going on in there, Sean?"

"I'm going to find out."

Sam stuck his face over it. "Wow. What's that wire do?"

Gary bopped Sam's head. "Let the guy concentrate, Sam."

"Oh. Yeah." Sam backed away to give Sean more room. "Sorry."

As Sean picked and probed, the swimmers watched as if he were performing surgery. The only sounds were the ragged singing on the other side of the kitchen door and Sam's nasal breathing.

Finally Gary stood up and ordered his two teammates, "Let's give the guy a break. Don't breath down his neck."

Sam and the other swimmer, a sophomore Sean didn't know, backed up respectfully. "Okay. Let's get out of here."

Gary herded them out the door, but Sam turned back in the doorway. "Hey, Sean, we're gonna go see a movie tomorrow night. You want to come?"

Sean waved a hand as if his work were too important to raise his head. "Give me a call."

"Okay."

"See ya," Gary called.

The door swished and swung. They were gone.

Sean pressed his hands onto the counter and stood tall. He wasn't really that involved in his work yet. He just wanted some distraction, some protection, in case Sam or Gary turned back at the last minute and taunted, "Hey, Egghead! Let's meet in the biology lab and watch those speeded-up pictures of plants growing. That's the only kind of movie you like. Ha. Ha. Ha." But the taunts didn't come. They hadn't for a long time.

Still, Sean's hands were trembling and he turned away from the counter to shake them out. He also wanted to check on Allie again. Cracking open the door, he scanned the area near the stage and the dance floor and the benches along the wall. An icy coolness spread over his skin. He didn't know what he was supposed to do about it, but Allie was gone.

Outside, the air was dark and damp. Allie dug her hands into her pockets and walked farther into the parking lot. A car started up near the fence, the headlights and the heat of the engine making a big cloud. Allie stopped. On cold days in New York City the subway sent a cloud of steam up through the grates in the street that looked a lot like that. Puffy. Thick. Strange. For a moment she shut her eyes and wrestled with the memory, then she kept on walking.

All her friends were trying so hard. Too hard. When Allie looked in Celia's blue-green eyes she was frightened by what she saw there . . . how important it was to Celia that Allie be somebody important and popular. It was almost as if Celia couldn't face the fact that the best friend she'd shared most of her life with had turned out to be a big zero.

30

"Let's face it," Allie mumbled to herself as she walked, "I'm nothing."

Why didn't her friends see that she would only disappoint them? Just like she had disappointed her parents . . . and her teachers . . . and everyone else who expected her to be someone wonderful and important. That was one thing New York City had taught her. Unlike Meg and Nick and Celia and Sean, she wasn't brilliant or talented or beautiful or clever or special in any way whatsoever.

Allie went halfway up the steps that connected the parking lot to the tennis courts. She sat down. The concrete was cold and the dampness quickly seeped through her skirt, but it was a safe pocket of darkness, so she stayed. She pulled her jacket more tightly around herself and ran her fingers lightly over the letters. NO FUTURE. She'd bought it in New York because she knew it would drive her parents crazy and that's exactly what they deserved for dragging her out there. She bought it to prove to her classmates there that she knew she was different from them and she didn't care.

In New York her parents had sent her to a school called Thorton, a small private school where all the other kids seemed as close as she, Meg, and Celia had once been. From the first day Allie knew it was hopeless. The Thorton girls wore loafers and faded khakis, ponytails, and no makeup. She'd thought that kids in New York would be wild and adventuresome, but they eyed her showy hats and Day-Glo clothes with suspicion.

The worst part had been the classes them-

31

selves. Allie knew she wasn't dumb, but she'd never been interested or excited by school. At Redwood, she could coast by, and, aside from her parents and sometimes Sean, no one bugged her about spacing out in class or coming home with C's.

That was not the way it was at Thorton. Kids laughed when she didn't know who Tolstoy was, snickered and rolled their eyes when she didn't have the facts to join in their debates about history or government. No wonder that, by the end, she hated going to school so much she'd cut and sit on the apartment rooftop instead.

Thinking about it made Allie woozy. She hugged her arms around her middle, leaned her cheek on her shoulder, and let her hair fall over her face. Light footsteps were tapping up from the bottom of the staircase but Allie didn't bother to see who was running by. She let the mist and the darkness surround her.

The footsteps were soft and quick, someone in tennis shoes and in a hurry. When they got to the very top, it was quiet, and then they started back down. Now the steps were slower, louder, heavier.

"Allie?"

Allie raised her head as a flash of adrenaline raced from her toes to her fingertips to the roots of her dyed hair. A boy with a narrow, angular face was backlit by the lights from the tennis courts. He wore an old baseball jacket and carried a canvas shoulder bag. Between the halo of light behind him and the heavy mist he looked like one of his own photographs.

"L.P.?"

She wondered when she would see him again. Everything went into slow motion as he climbed down a few more steps and let his bag drop onto the concrete. He stared at her, his brow getting more wrinkled and worried the longer he looked.

L.P. had changed in the six months since she'd last seen him. He'd filled out a little, his hair was longer and combed back smoothly. He wasn't wearing glasses, and from the way his eyes seemed so dark and big she guessed that he'd gotten contacts.

But it wasn't really the way he looked that was so different. It was the way he carried himself, the stillness and steadiness with which he stood there. He made no move to get closer.

"Are you going to the dance?" Allie said. That was all she could think of to say. Her heart was pounding so hard she thought it would burst.

L.P. looked toward the campus as if he'd forgotten that such a thing as a high school dance existed. "No. I came to get some photo stuff I left in my locker."

Of course. L.P. was a senior now. He didn't bother with silly dances. Allie shifted and squirmed, then looked off toward the street.

L.P. didn't budge. "I wondered when I'd run into you."

Allie's chest began to heave, but she held back the tears. Of course he was thinking the same thing she was. That's why they'd once been so close. But it was all gone now. She'd last talked to him right before Christmas when, after he'd planned and saved all fall to come and visit her, she'd told him to stay home. And she couldn't explain why she didn't want to see him because she didn't know herself. All she knew was that he wouldn't love her anymore, because there was nothing left to love.

L.P. folded his arms over his chest. He did not smile. "So, how were your last few months in New York?"

"Great," Allie answered much too quickly.

"You miss it?"

Allie shrugged, biting her lower lip to keep it from trembling. "Oh, yeah. A lot."

"Really."

"It's so dull here."

"I guess."

"Small town. You know."

"Sure."

When she didn't say anything else, L.P. knelt down and unbuckled his bag, as if the only reason he'd stopped was to look for something inside. He carefully filed through a stack of photographs, then opened a small yellow box, pulling out slides one at a time and holding each up to the light.

Allie watched his steady, purposeful hands. She wanted to tell him how much she'd missed him. How every day she'd thought about the museum trips they'd taken together, the movies they'd shared, the hours they'd walked and walked in the woods behind her house. She wanted to tell him how many times she'd thought about the soft warmth of his cheek and the wonderful, warm safeness of being in his arms. She said nothing.

34

L.P. closed the yellow box and stuck it in his shirt pocket. He buckled up his bag and stood up. "Well, welcome back."

Allie nodded.

He started up the stairs, his shoes making slow, shuffling sounds. Allie wondered if he'd turn back to look at her. But when she raised her head again there was nothing but the mist and the lights up on the tennis courts and the rattle of a car engine pulling into the lot.

"What's happening to me?" Allie cried, leaning her head against the banister and letting the tears pour down her face. Why hadn't she explained how she felt to L.P.? Why couldn't she explain it to her friends? Why did she just feel more and more lonely and out of place?

Trying to stop her tears, she dug in her pocket, pulling out a pack of cigarettes that she had bought her last day in New York. There were only two left, plus the matches stuck between the paper and the cellophane.

Allie lit up and sucked the smoke in. It made her throat sting and her head light, but she puffed as fast and as deeply as she could, working to inhale, making herself dizzier and dizzier.

Suddenly she heard footsteps again and held a hand in front of her face as she was hit with the beam of a flashlight.

"Who's that smoking?" intruded a sharp female voice.

Mrs. Weaver, the junior class adviser, was standing ten feet away. She was old, with thick legs and glasses on a chain around her neck. She had this disgusted expression on her face that

35

reminded Allie of her ex-classmates back at Thorton.

Instead of stamping the cigarette out or trying to hide it, Allie glared back and blew out a mouthful of smoke. She suddenly hated Mrs. Weaver, and her friends, and everything in Redwood Hills.

"There's no smoking on campus," Mrs. Weaver said. "You know that."

"No, I don't," Allie came right back. "I just transferred here."

Mrs. Weaver stepped closer. "Allie Simon?" She stared, scowling as she took in Allie's hair and clothes. "You were here last year. You know the rules. Put it out."

Allie let the cigarette drop, grinding it over and over with her heel for Mrs. Weaver's benefit. She started to get up.

"Put the butt in the trash can, please," Mrs. Weaver ordered.

Allie picked up the smashed filter and the squashed strands of tobacco. After she dropped it in the trash her fingers smelled dirty and burnt.

"Thank you," Mrs. Weaver chimed, leading the way to the cafeteria and not looking back.

"You're welcome," Allie mimicked to herself. She followed Mrs. Weaver along the lit walkways back to the cafeteria, slapping the ground with her heels. The last place she wanted to go was back to the dance, but she was trapped. Nick was giving her a ride and she didn't know how else she'd get home.

When they got inside, Allie hesitated in the hall. The noise and brightness were spilling out

36

from the cafeteria, but she couldn't make herself go in. Turning on her heel, she headed for the parking lot again, not sure where she would go once she got there. But she didn't get as far as the faculty lunchroom. Celia and Meg rushed out and surrounded her.

"Where did you go?" Celia cried. She acted as if Allie had just come back from being shipwrecked. "I was so worried about you."

"So was I," Meg confessed in a softer tone.

When Allie didn't answer, Celia took her hand and pulled her back down the hall. "Well, it doesn't matter," Celia cheered. "You're here now. Everything's okay."

"Sure," Allie muttered to herself, "everything's just great."

CHAPTER 4

TESTING ONE, TWO, THREE. . . .

Still back in the cafeteria kitchen, Sean bent over the microphone that The Crashers' lead singer had loaned him to check their speaker. He blew into it and listened, hoping to hear a clean rush of air. He puffed again and heard a smooth breeze. A sigh. A whoosh. Not a buzz or a crackle.

"All right!" he told himself. "Much better."

That was how Sean felt suddenly. So much better. Nearly perfect. Life without glitches or broken wires. He screwed the back on the speaker box and realized that for the first time since Allie'd come home, he really felt at ease.

Maybe it was having fixed the speaker. Maybe it was the way Sam and his friends had treated him. Maybe it was that Nick had just taken Allie home so he didn't have to worry about her anymore. Maybe it was that The Crashers were finally playing a decent tune. Whatever, it was the first time he'd felt this free and full of expectation since he'd stopped in San Francisco to buy Allie that thousand-year-old egg.

"Oooookay."

Sean was loading the equipment back on the cart when he was tempted by the weighty, cool feel of the microphone in his hand. He had to bring it up to his mouth again. It had been so long since he'd felt this good that he couldn't resist settling into the feeling and letting go.

"Hello dere," he said in a rumbly voice. The sound was low, quakey. The Crashers were much too loud for anyone outside to hear him. So Sean hummed a bar of music, moving his hips like he did when he sang with his records at home. An energy started to run inside him, a feeling he always got from good music or doing something he liked without worrying about what other people would think. He cut loose.

"I WOULD DO ANYTHING FOR YOU. . . ."

He held the cord in one hand and spun around. Head back, he stomped the ground.

"ANYTIME, ANYWHERE, YOU ARE THE WA-A-ONE."

He tossed the mike over his shoulder, spread his feet, and bent the strings on the neck of an imaginary guitar.

"TAANNNNG, WAAAOOOOOO, BOOOO-OIIIIIING. . . ."

"Hi."

Sean froze. He was posed with one fist thrust forward and his head bowed to the floor. His good mood crashed on the floor like a broken egg. He would have done anything at that moment — taken his PSAT's again, escorted Allie to the junior prom, given up his driving privileges for a month — not to be standing like he was, doing what he was doing, hearing what he had just heard. But there wasn't much he could do now but look up, pretend his face wasn't turning fiery red, and answer the "hi" that had definitely come from a girl.

"Uh," he cleared his throat as he lifted his eyes. "Hi."

"Am I interrupting something?" She smiled at him as if it were normal to seclude yourself in a cafeteria kitchen during a high school dance and pretend you were Bruce Springsteen.

"Oh, no. I was just testing this." He laughed. It was a very dumb laugh. "Just testing."

"Good."

"See, if I don't sing into it I can't tell if it's really fixed or not."

"That makes sense."

"It does?"

"Sure." She hiked herself up and sat on the metal counter.

"Oh. I guess it does."

Sean couldn't place her. The face was familiar — wide brown eyes, as many freckles as he, blonde hair in short curls, and a nose that you knew had sunburned and peeled every summer. But he had a hard time concentrating on her face because she was wearing a dress made of something pink and shiny that didn't have any straps. Her shoulders were totally bare. They had freckles, too, and all Sean wanted to do was touch those shoulders . . . play connect the dots with his fingers. His cheeks went burning hot and he started coiling the mike cord, praying she didn't know what he was thinking.

"You don't remember me, do you, Sean?"

Sean stared again, trying to focus on her eyes and her hair. He thought he'd recognize every girl he'd spoken more than two words to for the last five years. Without thinking, he could list the names of the ones he'd danced with — all six. And the two freshmen he'd actually gone on dates with were, unfortunately, unforgettable. The mike cord slipped out of his hand and spilled onto the floor.

"Brooke. Brooke Applebaum," she reminded him. She crunched down her skirt as if she were wearing an old housecoat instead of something suitable for the senior prom.

"Oh." Sean could barely speak. He felt so strange, as if he was standing on ice and if he made a wrong move his feet would fly out from under him.

"Paley's drivers' ed class?"

"Drivers' ed." The light finally turned on in Sean's head. "Oh, yeah! You sat behind me in those weird driving simulators. You used to fool around and make those car sounds while you drove."

Brooke nodded and laughed. "Yeah. I used to pretend that I was crashing into stuff or racing after criminals." She laughed again.

He kept staring at her. They'd been in that class together almost a year ago. She'd slimmed down, gotten her braces off. While his body and voice had changed so radically over the last two years, most girls he knew had stayed pretty much the same. Brooke had changed almost as much as he had. "You cut your hair."

She touched her curls. "Yeah."

"And you were the one who always argued with Paley because he hated having girls in auto shop."

"That's me."

"Did you ever take his class? Auto shop, I mean?"

"Not yet. But I'm going to senior year." Brooke took off a low-heeled pump and rubbed her foot. "I'm too busy with drama now."

"Oh." That must have been why Sean never saw her around the campus. The drama kids all ate lunch in Ms. Smith's new drama room and stayed for hours rehearsing after school.

"I build sets and work on the lighting. I'm stage managing the next show." She jumped down off the counter. Her dress was all wrinkled and kind of hiked up on the side. She still held one shoe. "That's why I came back here. Somebody said you were fixing the equipment, and I wanted to see what you were doing. See, as stage manager, I'll be in charge of making sure everything works right, so I'll need to know something about speakers and mikes."

Sean couldn't take his eyes off her as she sidled by him to peek in the toolbox. Her back was slightly tanned, and there were thin blonde wisps at the nape of her neck where her hair was cropped really short. She wore a tiny turquoise earring in each ear and a chain around her neck.

He watched her hands as she sorted through the band's tools with great interest. She dug to the bottom and pulled out an electric drill. The cord was long and curvy and pulled up about ten other things with it. Sean rushed over to help.

"Careful," he warned as a drill bit and a carton of nails spilled over onto the floor.

"Oh, sorry."

He leaned in to unhook the cord, but when he put his hand on the audiovisual cart it started to slide. He was afraid he might slide, too, when he jerked toward her. She spun around to face him. Suddenly almost dizzy, he tried to balance himself. There was nowhere to put his hands but on those bare, freckled shoulders.

Brooke was so close to him that he could feel her breath along his neck. Her shoe was still in one hand. Her other palm went flat against his chest. Now he was embarrassed at how hard his heart was pounding and wondered if she could feel it. He did not take his hands off her shoulders.

Her shoe dropped, clunk, onto the floor.

Sean stared into her brown eyes, which never left his. Then he did something he never, ever, EVER, in a million years would have thought he could have done. It was as if someone else temporarily stepped inside him, someone with ease and nerve and experience. He moved closer.

He closed his eyes.

He kissed her.

It was a short kiss. His mouth on hers, his hands on her beautiful shoulders and both of them standing very still. When he opened up his eyes she was staring up at him as if she couldn't believe it. He couldn't believe it, either.

He wondered if she'd haul off and slap him, like in the movies. But her arm didn't move. She kept gazing at him, her mouth open and her eyes huge.

At the exact same moment, they both dropped to their knees, scrambling to pick up the nails and the drill bit.

"I'll do it," Sean blurted. His voice came out all froggy and thick. "You'll get your dress dirty."

"I don't care. It's a dumb dress anyway."

"No, it's a great dress." It was like they were playing pick-up sticks.

"No. It's too fancy."

"No, it's not."

They continued to sort and collect. "Yes, it is. I always wear the wrong thing. If everybody's dressed up, then I wear overalls. If everyone's in jeans, I wear something like this."

"I still think it's beautiful."

"You do?" she asked, amazed.

All the nails were picked up. They slowly stood.

Sean swallowed hard. She was gazing up at him again. He wasn't sure exactly what was happening. All he knew was that he didn't want it to stop. He wanted to kiss her again, but unfortunately, that nervy person inside him had fled. They put the nails back in the toolbox and brushed off their hands.

When they were done Sean asked, "Do you still want to know about the speaker?" That was all he could think of to say.

"Maybe you could tell me about it some other time." The band finished a song. There were a few hoots and a smattering of applause. A slow tune started up. "Could we dance instead?" Brooke asked it straightforwardly, without a hint of coyness.

"Dance?"

"You don't want to?"

"Oh, no. I mean, yes, I'd love to dance. Sure."

"Okay." She walked slowly out of the kitchen. Sean pushed the cart behind her. He knew the cart was heavy — it had been heavy when he wheeled it in there, but now it felt as light as an empty baby stroller. He left it next to the band platform and joined Brooke on the floor.

His hands slid over her bare skin. He pulled her close and they moved very slowly.

"Are you cold?" he whispered.

She didn't answer, merely shook her head no.

They continued to dance, barely moving until the song ended. It was only then that Sean noticed with a smile that she was still wearing only one shoe.

Outside in the hall, Celia sat with little stacks of tickets lined up in front of her. She was supposed to be helping Meg count, but for the moment she wasn't sure how many tickets were in each stack or why she was even counting them.

"Cici, I have two hundred and twelve. Is that what you have?"

"Huh?"

"Dollars. I have two hundred and twelve dollars. You should have two hundred and twelve tickets. Do you?"

"I don't know. I lost count."

Celia went through the stacks one more time as the band launched into another set. The bass was starting to thump inside her head.

"Did Tim go home?" Meg asked as she stowed the money in a manila envelope.

"About fifteen minutes ago."

"It's too bad he has to live so far away." Celia's boyfriend had moved to Marin when his stepfather took custody of his kids the previous fall.

"You're telling me."

"Is everything okay with him and you?"

"Yeah. It's hard that we can't see each other very often, but other than that, we're okay."

Meg peered down the hall. "I wonder if Nick's coming back." She got up and balanced her foot on the edge of the table as if she were limbering before a race. "Did he say if he'd be back here after he took Allie home?"

"I don't think so."

For a moment Meg looked as preoccupied as Celia, then she laughed. "I should stop bugging you and let you count. Let me know when you're done." Meg went down to open the door to the quad and let in a cool, damp breeze.

Celia pushed the tickets around with a limp hand, but she was unable to keep the numbers in her head. Nothing much stuck in her head this last week except Allie. Even Tim had noticed. He'd wanted to talk about his new stepbrothers, and about how Celia was getting along with her mother, but she kept coming back to the same topic: Allie.

There was no way Tim could really understand because he was a senior, Celia'd decided. She'd given this a lot of thought over the week and realized that her frustration with Allie had to do with the fact that Allie'd flaked out just when they'd hit the pinnacle of high school life — junior year. The underclassmen all looked up to them now. The seniors had recently become too bored with high school or too panicked about the future to run things. The Class of '88 had influence, independence, and real power in the school, and her friends were the top group within the junior class. They were the leaders, like Meg; the top athletes, like Nick; the great students, like Sean; the style setters, like her. There was no reason to worry about the rich social girls like Whitney Hain anymore — between chasing college boys and sneaking into beer parties, they were as out of the picture as the seniors.

Why couldn't Allie realize that if she only made an effort, she could be part of it, too! Celia knew what it was like to be excluded, even to exclude yourself from things at school. She'd had plenty of experience being snubbed and made fun of because of her weird mother, who worked as a hairdresser downtown and dressed like a cheap sixteen-year-old. But she'd managed to jump back into things. She could deal with her mom now. She'd simply told her mom not to show up at school functions or even pick her up in the parking lot. And kids had eventually forgotten that her mom wore metallic miniskirts and lavender-streaked hair. That's what Allie had to do — change her image and put the past behind her. With a new look, a decent attitude, and her old friends at her side, the rest of the juniors would forgive and forget.

But it had to be soon. That was another thing Celia realized about junior year. She saw the terror on the senior's faces, the ones who hadn't thought about life after high school until they were suddenly being thrust into it. It was time to stop fooling around. This year life was starting to be for keeps.

"Celia. CICI."

Celia realized that she was still sitting there with a fist full of uncounted tickets when she felt Meg tug on her hair and heard banging on the window behind her. The beige walls and checkered linoleum came back into focus.

"I think I'm being asked to dance," Meg laughed.

Celia turned around. Patrick Delancie and Sam Pond were on the other side of the window, in the cafeteria. Sam was pushing Patrick against the glass, dancing behind him, motioning for Meg to join Patrick on the floor. Patrick flicked his long hair over his eyes to cover his embarrassment.

"Come on, Cici. We have to rescue Patrick from that maniac. You can finish counting later."

Meg pulled Celia up. Just managing to stuff the tickets into the cigar box, Celia followed Meg back into the dance.

As soon as they got inside, Patrick took Meg's

money envelope and offered to deliver it to Mrs. Weaver for her.

"He'll be right back," Sam reminded Meg with a demonic laugh. "Don't go away."

"Get lost, Sam," Meg teased.

Celia stared at the dance floor, watching the back of Patrick's Farm Aid T-shirt disappear into the blue and green light. Suddenly she spotted something that made a new part of her brain open up, a part that miraculously was not filled up with thoughts of Allie. But this new entry was just as disturbing. "Who's Sean dancing with?"

Meg was unbraiding her long hair and shaking it over her shoulder. She had the rubber band in her mouth. "I don't know."

Celia could only see them from the back — the girl's naked shoulders and the way Sean was hugging her, like he'd just proposed marriage. Sean spun her around and Celia gasped. "Oh, my God, it's Applebomber."

"Who?"

"Brooke Applebaum. Everybody calls her Applebomber. She was in my history class. If everybody did an oral report, she'd turn in a written one. If we all did essays, she'd build a model. She's really weird. She always walks around the halls with a hammer in her overalls. I think she took auto shop or something."

"They look kind of cute together."

"Cute? That dress looks like she's at the Miss America pageant."

Meg waved to Patrick, who was on his way

back over. "I think somebody stole one of her shoes."

"I told you, she's weird."

But Meg was no longer listening. Patrick was pulling her onto the floor and she was playfully fighting him, her long hair flying in bouncy, even waves.

Celia continued to stare at Sean and Brooke. With every beat of the bass her head thunked even harder. Applebomber? Sean couldn't be serious. They hadn't spent three years convincing Redwood High that Sean Pendleton was a cool guy to have him fall for an out-and-out bizarro like Brooke Applebomber.

Celia's head was really screaming now. She wished that Tim were still there, or Nick, or someone with some sense. She hugged the box of tickets to her chest and threw one last concerned look at Sean pressed close to the weirdo in the Miss America dress.

CHAPTER 5

The inside of the bus smelled like dust and potato chips and sounded like a big party in a small room. Juniors pried windows open, but it just let in the exhaust from the other buses warming up next to them. The seats were cracked and the floor was sticky, but Sean found it all indescribably beautiful.

It was Monday, after third period, and the junior class was headed on a field trip to see a play in San Francisco. Mrs. Weaver climbed on and barked for quiet. Sean sat up. Her voice, which usually made him feel as if he had a serious case of poison oak, today caused a mere tingle. Nick, who sat next to him, groaned.

"Quiet down, everybody," Mrs. Weaver snapped. She had her glasses on the tip of her nose, looking over them to see the juniors, and down through them to check her clipboard. "How many empty seats left on this bus?"

51

Sean shot up. They'd loaded the buses according to third period class. He, Nick, and Meg all had physiology together, so they'd been shuttled onto this bus. Celia, who had business math in the room next door, was on it, too — she sat up front with Meg. He'd seen Allie climbing onto one of the other buses, but he hadn't seen Brooke. He could only pray that whatever class Brooke had third period, she might still be out there looking for a seat. Any moment she could walk up those steps onto his bus.

"There's two seats over here," Sean pointed out, falling over the girl in front of him. Nick pulled him back by the hem of his gas station shirt. He almost landed in Nick's lap.

"You're sure in a good mood." Nick was shuffling a few typed papers, reading them over.

Sean smiled and shrugged. He wasn't sure what to say, even to his best friend, or what to make of this strange state he was in. Since the dance, he'd barely slept — yet he wasn't tired. He'd had to force down his protein malts — he wasn't hungry. Yesterday he'd had so much energy, he'd reprogrammed the computer for his parents' bicycle store, found three new routes up the back of Capitola Mountain, and ironed his entire collection of bowling and gas station shirts.

Nick's brow was furrowed. He had a pencil in his mouth and his usual easy confidence was missing. "Sean, could you look at this and tell me if it all makes sense to you?" Nick handed the papers to him.

"Sure." Sean took the pages and tried to stay seated as the engine rumbled and roared. *Where was Brooke*? He's looked for her before school that morning, but he didn't know if she walked or took the bus or where her homeroom was. She was probably already on one of these buses, but where, and which one?

Why hadn't he just called her over the weekend! He'd given himself a million excuses. He was already going out with Sam and the guys on Saturday night. If he wasn't going to ask her out, what would he say to her? It seemed too early to call for next weekend. Besides, he wasn't sure what he should ask her to do, where he should take her. Face it. He was scared. Terrified. He'd never felt like this before. Just thinking about Brooke made his heart beat so fast he thought he'd faint.

The bus pulled out and Sean was jerked back into his seat. As they wound around the side streets, past Albertson's Market and the tire store and the downtown mall, he read Nick's paper. That calmed him a little. It was an essay about running called "Life on the Fast Track." Nick had recently become interested in writing, especially about sports. Sean thought he was a pretty good writer and had been encouraging him to submit something to the school newspaper.

"Now this is the one you should send in to *The Guardian*," Sean said.

Nick cocked his head and his green eyes got an uncharacteristically shy look. "I already did."

"You did! Are they going to print it?"

"They're letting me know."

"That's great that you finally sent one in!" Sean was brimming over with affection. Nick

53

had done it — written an article and actually submitted it to the paper. He wanted to hug Nick, to cry, to announce it to the whole bus. Suddenly all his friends, even Allie, seemed so wonderful to him he could hardly contain himself. He even liked Mrs. Weaver. "It's a great essay, Nick. I bet they print it. It's terrific."

"Thanks." Nick looked pleased and a little embarrassed. He took back his essay and looked it over again.

As the bus drove on, past a grove of nut trees and a roadside vegetable stand, Sean had the urge to spread his arms and break into song, like in some corny musical. He found new beauty in everything — the color of the tomatoes and the peppers, the graceful arc of the street lamps, the stark simplicity of the signs along the highway.

When his heart started skipping again, he wondered if he was going crazy. After all, he'd only danced with Brooke, and kissed her, of course. He'd never forget that. But he hadn't seen her since he'd walked her to her car Friday night. Maybe when he did see her again she'd ignore him. Maybe she didn't like him back. Maybe the whole thing was just in his head.

Sean decided he needed advice. He'd ask Nick. If there was anyone who knew about girls, it was his best friend. "You go out with Darcy this weekend?"

Nick nodded without looking up. "Does 'flying like an eagle' seem right to you — in the second paragraph?"

"Sure. What'd you do? With Darcy, I mean. Where'd you take her?"

"To a party. How about 'fly like a dove'? Is that better?"

"Sure. How are things going with Darcy?"

"She's okay. I guess eagle's the right word."

"Mm. Yeah." Sean started to feel self-conscious. He wondered if Nick had ever felt the way he did right now. Tons of girls pursued Nick, and it seemed to Sean that Nick gave in because it was easier than saying no.

"Oh," Nick remembered as the bus made a sharp turn and chugged up the freeway on-ramp, "can we study together for the physiology midterm? I think Meg wants to. I hear it's going to be a killer, a definite all-nighter."

Sean could only nod his head because his voice was caught in his throat. As they surged onto the freeway another Redwood bus zoomed past and pressed against the window was the blonde-haired, freckle-faced girl who had not been off his mind for more than five minutes in the last two-and-a-half days. Brooke saw him.

SHE WAVED!

Sean threw himself forward with such velocity that he smashed his nose into the glass. He barely felt it. He waved back and decided that if Nick had never experienced this feeling, well, it was just too bad for Nick.

The play was Shakespeare's *The Tempest*, the story of a magician and his daughter who lived on an island with strange spirits and creatures. A ship got wrecked and some other men came to the island, including a young one who fell in love with the magician's daughter. In the end the daughter married the young man, and they left the island and her father set his favorite spirit free.

The play was long, and in poetry, and while most of the juniors had liked it, a few had napped or whispered their way through it. Downstairs, during the first act, three boys had thrown candy and paper airplanes. Mrs. Weaver and the other teachers were so furious at those three boys that they'd barely let anyone leave their seats — kids practically had to get a pass to go to the bathroom during intermission. Now the play was over, and they were still being forced to sit and wait.

Most everybody was chattering, leaning over chairs and aisles, finding out who the three boys were and what was going to happen to them. Not Allie. She was pitched forward on the balcony railing, gazing down at the trees and the grass hut and scattered flower petals that were still on-stage. There was no curtain so it was easy to stay lost in that magical world down there. For her, the last two-and-a-half hours had been beautiful. For once she hadn't thought about L.P. or Celia or Thorton School or any of it. This was the first time since she'd come home that life had made sense.

Painful reality returned in the form of Mrs. Weaver's voice. "Before we get back on the bus," Mrs. Weaver commanded, "we are all meeting in the lobby for a lecture on theater manners." Everyone moaned. "I'd like all of you in the balcony to wait and let the students downstairs get settled first."

Allie leaned way over to watch the juniors below file out. At first she'd been disappointed when her busload was sent to the balcony, so far from the stage. But now she was glad. Her old friends were down below and couldn't demand that she sit with them or socialize with their crowd. And she'd gotten to sit in the balcony front row, where she could lean on the railing with no one in front of her. She'd been able to watch as if nothing and nowhere else in the world existed.

Allie was still lost in the magic of the play, when someone tapped her shoulder. She gave the slightest look back and let her hair cover her face.

"Aren't you a good friend of Sean Pendleton's?" asked the girl sitting behind her. She was wearing pink overalls and holding a flashlight pen.

Allie nodded, then went back to leaning over the balcony. She was surprised when she felt another tap. Lately she'd gotten pretty good at sending leave-me-alone messages. But this girl didn't seem to notice or care.

"My name's Brooke. I think we were in choir together freshman year." Brooke smiled. "I wondered if you'd seen where Sean was sitting."

"Downstairs somewhere. I don't know."

"Oh, shoot." Brooke squeezed over Allie to look down. "I'll never find him. Do you remember me from choir? I think we sang in the same section."

"I've blocked choir out. I always sang off-tune."

Brooke laughed. She plopped back and pulled

a big knapsack up from under her seat. When she opened it to put back her flashlight pen, Allie found herself turning around to look.

"I sang off-key, too," Brooke said as she sorted through her bag. There was a hammer in there, and a wrench, and some kind of meter. "Not only that, I used to get carried away and come in at the wrong time. Finally Mrs. Barlow asked me just to move my lips."

Allie suddenly did remember Brooke, and as she did she found it strange that Brooke would want to remind her. Brooke had been chunky then, and for a short time wore one of those awful headgears to straighten her teeth. Some kids had laughed at her, but it never went very far because Brooke never let it bother her. The Brooke who sat behind her now was slim and pretty, but the self-assurance was the same, as if she knew what she was doing and she didn't care if other people agreed with her or not.

"It's funny how some people don't recognize me from sophomore and freshman years."

"You're lucky," Allie grumbled. "I wish people didn't recognize me."

"No chance of that. Not with your friends. Everybody knows who they are. That's how I found out you were an old friend of Sean's. Everybody knows your crowd."

Allie turned her back to Brooke again. "They're not my crowd."

Mrs. Weaver, who'd been standing with her arms outstretched like a human stop sign, was now gesturing for them to get moving.

58

"Did you like the play?" Brooke asked as they waited to reach the aisle.

"I loved it," Allie gushed. Then she looked away, embarrassed. She had guarded her feelings for so long that she didn't feel comfortable letting Brooke know just how much the play had affected her. But there was something about Brooke that made it hard to stay hidden and defensive.

"Me, too," Brooke sighed, hugging her bag against her overalls. "I thought Caliban was the best. And Ariel."

Caliban was the monster on the island that everyone made fun of. At times his anger had reminded Allie of her own frustration. Ariel was the good spirit who could fly and fool people and make magic. Allie had loved both of those characters, too. "They were both pretty weird."

Brooke laughed. "I always like the weird characters best. I guess that's because I'm weird." She said it as if it was something to be proud of.

"Come on, don't dawdle," Mrs. Weaver was barking. "Let's get downstairs."

Allie and Brooke were bottled up between the hallway to the stairs and a fire door. The door was ajar and let in a breeze that made Allie shiver. "I can't believe we all have to get yelled at just because of three jerks." Thinking about a lecture on manners was turning this wonderful afternoon into something dreary and depressing, like every other day of her junior year. "She sure knows how to ruin a decent day."

"I know." Brooke stared at Allie until her brown eyes opened wider and she stepped back, easing open the door. Outside was a fire escape and narrow metal steps leading down to the ground. "Maybe we can keep it a good afternoon."

"What do you mean?"

Brooke put a finger to her lips. "How'd you like to go look backstage instead of listening to that lecture?"

Allie didn't have time to attempt coolness. Her excitement exploded through. "Could we really do that! How?"

"Shhh!" Brooke held Allie back, letting other kids go ahead of them. "I bet everybody'll be in the lobby for at least ten minutes." She looked down the stairs. "So why don't we go down the fire stairs and peek around the stage and then join everybody when they get out of the lobby. Do you want to?"

Allie didn't have to think about it. To actually be down on the stage, to touch, see, and smell it — she would practically have thrown herself off the balcony. "Okay."

They waited for Mrs. Weaver to turn her back and fled down the metal steps, their feet tap-tap-tapping all the way to the bottom. They landed in an alley that looked more like the driveway to an underground garage than the side of a theater.

Brooke hurried toward the back of the building, but Allie had to stop for a moment and look out at the street. It was a cool, clear day and she could smell the ocean underneath the heavy car exhaust. On the corner a cable car rattled to a stop, picked up a few passengers who hung on the outside, and rattled on. People rushed by three-deep along the sidewalk and it reminded Allie of New York City, but without the edge or the strangeness.

"Come on," Brooke urged.

Allie ran. She wasn't sure why, but it was as if the hood that she'd been wearing over her brain were being lifted. She followed Brooke around the side of the building and stopped, staring at an entrance that read STAGE DOOR.

Brooke knocked.

"You were away for a while, right?"

Allie nodded. "In New York City."

"Wow. I'd like to hear about that sometime. You must have seen lots of plays there."

"No." Allie wondered why she hadn't, except that her parents weren't interested in the theater, and after the first few weeks they were so upset with the way she was acting that they refused to let her do anything on her own.

The door opened. An old man wearing a plaid cap, with a cigarette hanging out of his mouth, stood in front of them. He squinted from the smoke and didn't seem to notice when the ash tumbled down on his shirt.

"Hi," Brooke said. "We're from Redwood High, the school group that just saw the play. Can we just look around backstage? Please. I promise we won't touch anything."

He looked skeptical.

"I'm the stage manager for the drama club. I really want to see how a real theater looks."

Allie was sure he'd say no, but then something in his face softened and he motioned them in.

"I'll give you two minutes," he told them. "I'll be watching you."

Brooke and Allie thanked him about ten times and rushed past a room full of wigs on Styrofoam heads and two racks of costumes. It all smelled of sawdust, sweat, and makeup. When they stepped onto the back of the stage, Allie let loose with a giggle, a hint of her old wacky laugh. On one side were ropes heading up to a high, high ceiling and attached to sandbags on the bottom. On the other were pieces of black curtain and an entrance onto the stage itself.

Allie led the way. "Brooke, look."

Brooke, who had her head cocked back to see the lights and catwalks overhead, gasped.

They both stared not at the stage, but at the house beyond, rows and rows of red velvet seats going on forever. There was something eerie and wonderful about all those empty seats. Allie could instantly fill every one with her imagination.

"This makes our theater at school look like a shoebox," Brooke whispered as they tiptoed to the lip of the stage. They both held their arms in close to their bodies, careful not to touch the trees, which up close looked flat and cartoony, or disturb a single rose petal lying on the stage floor.

"So you're a stage manager?" Allie asked when they reached the edge. She was truly curious. It had been a while since she'd been curious about anything.

"Yeah. For the drama club."

"What do you do?"

"I run the rehearsals. And I help make sure it all comes together — between Ms. Smith, the actors, and the techies. I also take stage crew seventh period so I can build sets." Brooke turned to look at Allie. "You know, if you really like all this, you should come paint scenery or audition for the next play this Friday. It's open to the whole school."

"Really?" The idea of trying for the play made Allie suddenly hopeful. She'd read a few plays out loud at Thorton. Those were the only times she'd been able to escape from herself or see any respect on her classmates' faces.

But suddenly a gate clanged shut inside Allie and her hopefulness fled. The seats no longer looked mysterious and enticing. Now they were just empty chairs with aisles, down which a stern, thick-limbed woman was storming.

"Is that you, Allie Simon?" Mrs. Weaver was demanding, rushing toward them from the lobby. "You are going to drive me crazy. I should have known."

Brooke immediately clambered onto the edge of the stage and jumped down in front of the first row. "It was my idea, Mrs. Weaver," she admitted. "I wanted to see what the stage looked like."

Allie lowered herself down next to Brooke while Mrs. Weaver lectured, "Brooke, you were supposed to go down to the lobby with everyone else. I know that you are interested in drama and that you'd be the last one to need a lesson in theater manners, but we could have left on the bus without you."

"Allie's really interested, too — " Brooke tried to say.

Weaver cut her off and pointed toward the lobby. "Brooke, please go join the rest of your classmates."

Brooke took a few steps, then turned back to wait for Allie.

Mrs. Weaver waved Brooke on. "I'd like to talk to Allie alone."

Brooke gave Allie a regretful stare. Finally she turned and walked slowly up the aisle.

"Allie, what do you have to say for yourself?"

"Not a thing." Allie slid a play program back and forth with her boot. She kicked it.

"You're not going to tell me you didn't know the rules this time?"

Allie kicked another program. It flew in the air and landed on a seat a few rows back. "Nope."

"Since you've been back you've been a real pain, you know that."

"Whatever you say, Mrs. Weaver." Allie was about to kick a third program when Mrs. Weaver grabbed her arm.

"Come on. You'll sit with me on the way home."

Mrs. Weaver pulled Allie up the aisle and through the kids in the lobby. Everybody stared as they jerked past. When they finally got outside, there was a huddle of well-dressed, good-looking kids who also turned to watch Allie's misery. And right in front, hands on her hips, looking shocked and angry, was Celia.

Sean hadn't been able to locate Brooke during the lobby lecture, so he'd made a point of being the first one out to the bus. At least if he'd been able to set eyes on her, to smile, to wave, he might have felt as if life was worth living. But to know that she was in the same building and he hadn't even seen her. . . . It was more than he could endure.

He sat in his seat, his forehead leaning on the window. His body felt limp, drained. Maybe Brooke had left at intermission. Maybe she was right next to him, but hiding because she didn't want to see him! Oh, why hadn't he called her over the weekend? He was making himself loony.

Nick was sitting next to him, reading his article again, then staring thoughtfully into space with a pencil under his chin. He looked so purposeful — the uncreased polo shirt, canvas watchband, tanned arms, square jaw. Sean decided to explain everything — name, details, feelings. Even if Nick had never felt this way himself, he'd surely have some insight into how to handle it. But just then Nick got up and gathered his books.

"You don't mind, do you Nick?" Celia said to her cousin. She was standing over Nick. She seemed nervous, fidgeting and flicking back her blonde hair. "It's important."

"I don't care." Nick punched Sean's shoulder, then made his way forward to sit in Celia's old seat, next to Meg.

Celia slid in next to Sean. She folded her arms over her pale yellow sweater. "Did you hear what just happened? Everybody's talking about it."

"You mean Josh, Ken, and David getting detention?" They were the three boys who'd thrown candy.

Celia rolled her eyes as if Sean was being intentionally dense. "No! I mean what happened to Allie."

Sean shook his head. Since he'd met Brooke he'd kind of forgotten about Allie.

"Maria says it's all because of your friend Brooke. It was her idea."

Brooke! Something that felt like an army of ants ran up his spine. His friend Brooke! How did Celia know Brooke was "his friend"? What was Brooke doing with Allie?

"I should have said something to you at the dance," Celia said, shaking her head. "This is partly my fault. I should have stopped it right away."

"What are you talking about?!!"

Sean sank into his seat as Celia chattered on about Brooke being a nerd and an oddball and how she'd just gotten Allie into terrible trouble. Surely Sean wasn't interested in a girl that *everyone* knew was a weirdo. And of course he didn't like someone who had intentionally hurt one of THEM.

Sean couldn't absorb all of it; there was too much chatter going on inside his own head. All he knew was that he'd fallen in love. Madly, deeply, insanely in love. And one of his oldest friends was telling him it was with the wrong person.

CHAPTER 6

Nick grabbed and tickled. Meg screamed with laughter. Sean put his head down on the kitchen table and covered his ears.

"Nick! Nick, stop," Meg was giggling. She gasped for breath and pried Nick's hands away from her waist. "I told you it was a great article — what more do you want?"

Nick wrapped his arms more tightly, enjoying the push-pull and the sound of her muffled laughter against his neck. "Admit it. I'm a great writer."

"You're a great egomaniac."

"*The Guardian* begged me to print my article."

"I'm sure they did."

"They did. At school today."

They were in Nick's kitchen, surrounded by copper pots, antique dishes, two Cuisinarts, and stack after messy stack of physiology notes. Meg laughed and punched, her clear blue eyes still sending those I-dare-you, I'm-not-ready-to-give-in-yet messages. Nick finally put her down. "After I begged them to consider it for an entire week, they finally begged me to let them print it."

"Aha! The truth at last." Meg caught her breath, pushing long strands of hair out of her eyes. "Well, for a first try," she said coyly, "I'd say," she paused, "that it's definitely, um . . . better than average."

"Better than average." Nick moaned and held his head. "Sean, did you hear that? Better than average?"

Sean shrugged.

"Okay, it's good," Meg said as quickly as she could. "It's actually very good, and you should write a lot more. But you'd better not get a big head."

Nick grinned and stuck out his hand, which Meg shook. He wasn't sure why, but her approval of his new venture was very important.

"Sean, what do you think?"

"I told you before," Sean growled, "it's great." He was slumped over the table buried in notes, anatomy diagrams, and open textbooks. He had one hand in his hair while the other turned the page of his lab book. "I thought we were supposed to be studying for this midterm."

Meg looked back to Nick as she marched across the kitchen to sit back down next to Sean. Neither of them knew why Sean was so grouchy, although Nick figured Meg would make a bigger deal out it than he would. Sure enough, Meg leaned over and fluttered her fingers along the top of Sean's back.

Sean pushed her hand away.

"Sorry," Meg said, raising her hands. "I didn't mean to touch your delicate deltoid."

Sean passed her an anatomy diagram. "It's not my deltoid, it's my trapezius. If you'd start studying and stop screwing around, you'd know that."

"Thank you, Dr. Science." Meg cast one more look toward Nick before flopping down over her notebook.

It was clear that Sean was going through something — Monday he'd been acting as if he'd won the lottery, and just as suddenly he'd turned into Mr. Gloom. But Nick figured it would pass. Sean was probably stressed-out over midterms. Maybe he was down because the rain had come back. Or maybe he was just going through some mysterious identity crisis, like Allie.

It was hard for Nick to deal with his friends' moods lately: Celia's anxiety, Allie's confusion, Sean's sudden sadness. He was grateful that at least things with Meg were finally normal. Never, since middle school, had he and Meg had a relationship that was so calm and uncomplicated. That's what Nick liked about junior year. Lack of complication. When he was an underclassman he'd worried so much about his friends, his image, whether or not his team was going to win, what his father thought of him, if he was living up to his brothers' examples, that he could barely stand it. It was the same thing with girls. But now he realized he could hang out with a girl, have fun, and it didn't have to mean anything special.

Feeling relaxed and sure, he scooped his book off the counter and walked over to join Sean and

Meg. Something caught his eye in the backyard. At first he thought it was Hughie, his dog, trampling the flowers. Then he thought maybe it was Allie — he'd seen her walking in the woods behind their houses a few times since she'd been back. But as the yellow raincoat and glossy hair got closer he saw that it was Darcy. She bounced up to the window and rapped on the glass. Sean sighed loudly as he and Meg lifted their heads. Nick hurried to open the back door.

"Hi," Darcy squealed, panting slightly. She reached up to kiss Nick. Her riding boots were dappled with wet blades of grass and left marks on the floor as she walked over to Sean and Meg. "I knocked and knocked at the front door but nobody answered."

"My mom's not home yet," Nick told her. "I guess we didn't hear you."

She leaned over Sean and peered down at his anatomy diagram. "Eww. Gross. Are you studying?"

Sean slammed his book shut. "Not anymore."

Meg looked up. "Hi, Darcy."

"Oh, I'm sorry. I didn't mean to interrupt you." Darcy shook her hair and peeled off her raincoat. She obviously had no intention of leaving right away. "Meg, I'm so glad you're here. I was going to wait until the next junior meeting to talk to you, but this is even better."

"Oh?"

Nick was standing behind Darcy and she pulled him in, lacing his arms around her waist. "I just heard from the people at Bradley College and they're sending someone to College Day — an alumnus who lives in Petaluma." Darcy grinned so hard her dimples looked like two oil puddles. "I found out the ski season there is almost five months. I can't wait."

"Hey, Darcy," Meg mentioned, eager to change the subject, "what do you think about Nick's article getting in the paper?"

Darcy spun around to face Nick. "Oh, Nick. You didn't really send that article in, did you?" Before he had a chance to answer, she lectured, "Just as long as you don't stop running track to have more time to write. That would be the dumbest thing you could do."

"You were thinking of dropping track to write for the paper?" Meg asked, shocked. "You never told me that."

Nick looked uncomfortable. "I haven't decided. I've just been thinking about it."

"I mean, it might be a good idea," Meg reasoned. "It's not like you haven't spent half your high school life on that athletic field. I'm just surprised you didn't tell me."

Nick stepped toward Meg. "Well, I don't tell you everything, you know."

"I know. I just thought, something important like that."

"Actually, I wanted to talk about it with you, I just couldn't find the right time."

Darcy stepped between them, spreading her arms like an umpire calling safe. "What is it with you two?" she demanded, showing a little temper. She quickly regained control and said to Meg, "There's no need for you to worry. Nick's not going to stop running track."

"Okay." Meg handed Sean's lab book to him and started gathering her own things. "Nick should do whatever he wants."

"And what he wants is to run track." Darcy kissed Nick's cheek.

Sean stood up and slung his book bag over his shoulder. "Look, guys, since what *I* want is to pass this test and what Mag wants is to someday get into medical school, we'd better go someplace where we can study."

"Wait, you want to be a doctor?" Nick asked Meg, stopping her. "When did you decide that? How come you didn't tell me?"

Meg pulled on her blazer as Sean led the way out. "I haven't decided. I'm just thinking about it. Besides, I don't tell you everything, either." She stopped in the doorway. "Darcy, why don't you guys call Celia. She and Patrick are handling the last minute tables for College Day. Our midterm is that same afternoon so I won't have time. Okay?"

"Come on, Meg," urged Sean. He was half in the rain, jangling his van keys, his parka over his head. "Let's go."

Meg hesitated in the doorway, looking back at Nick. "I'm coming. 'Bye. See you guys at bowling Saturday night."

The damp wind came in, then the back door closed. Sean and Meg tromped back across the window, and they were gone.

"I can't believe she's serious about being a doctor," Darcy sighed, leaning over the table to watch the van pull out. "Who wants to stay in college for ten years, or whatever it is. Yuck."

Nick stared at the books still open on the table, a scarf that Meg had left behind, the plate with half-eaten sandwiches, and the three empty juice glasses. The ease that he prized so much was suddenly gone, and he found himself wishing that Darcy would be gone, too. It bugged him that Meg would have made an important decision like that without telling him. And he found himself wondering now why Sean was acting so strangely.

Darcy put her hand on his shoulder. "Nick, why don't you put all this stuff away and come with me to Marci's. They rented tons of videos. That's why I came by, to pick you up."

He took a deep breath. The last thing he was in the mood to do was party on a Thursday night. But he didn't want to make a big deal out of it.

"Why don't I call Celia first," he said, stalling for time.

"Oh, yeah. Good idea."

He dialed Celia's number and gave her the info about Bradley. But before he could hang up Celia went into a muffled tone, like she didn't want her mother to hear. She whispered, "Nick, my mom got that dumb College Day invitation in the mail and she keeps saying she wants to go. Is your mom coming, so I can just say I'm going with her instead?"

"I don't think so." Nick rubbed his forehead, trying to smooth out the thoughts that were starting to knot him up inside. His father, a California state senator, had been in Sacramento all week and his mother was planning some fund-raising luncheon. "They're too busy."

"Shoot," Celia continued. "Well, if my mom

shows up, I'll die. I'll just have to tell her. Absolutely no way is she going to come."

"What's the big deal, Cici?" Nick couldn't believe Celia was still so hung up about her mother.

"You wouldn't understand. Say hi to Darcy. Tell her I'll see you guys at the bowling alley Saturday night."

"Right."

" 'Bye."

Nick put the phone down. The complications were coming back and he didn't like it. He sunk down in the kitchen chair.

Darcy came up behind him and leaned on his shoulders. "So, are we going to Marci's?"

"Huh?"

"Marci's. I heard she has the new Bangles video."

"Oh. Yeah. Sure." Nick could think of a million ways he'd rather spend the evening — write, lift weights, watch the rain, study, sit in front of the TV with Hughie. He'd even rather sweep out their old childhood tree house, something he hadn't done in ages.

But he didn't say that to Darcy. It was easier not to.

By the time Sean got home he was too angry to study. He had dropped Meg off at her house, then braked in front of Celia's, which was next door to Meg's. He stared through the dusk at the patchy grass and the torn lawn chair and that weird Astroturf in front of Celia's door and got angrier and angrier. He could see Celia through the living room drapes. She was facing her mother with her hands on her hips, and it looked as if they were arguing. He bet if he turned off his motor he'd be able to hear their voices.

OOOh, how he wanted to burst out of that van and start arguing with them. He would have taken Celia's mother's side, no matter what the fight was about. That's how mad he was at Celia for the things she'd said about Brooke. But more than that, he was furious at himself for listening, for avoiding Brooke all week just because Celia said she was a nerd or a geek or whatever stupid name was in use this semester.

Somehow seeing Darcy and Nick had pushed him to the brink. He hated the way Darcy told Nick he should run track . . . should go to this college . . . shouldn't do this or that. He didn't understand why Nick put up with it. Of course, wasn't he just as bad, listening to Celia and letting her run his life, regardless of what he really thought or felt?

"Enough is enough," he said, ready to twist off the motor, walk right up to Celia's door, and tell her exactly what he thought.

He stopped himself. Why did he have to say anything to Celia at all? This was none of her business. This didn't involve anyone but him and Brooke.

With a new sense of purpose, and the beginning of some hope in his heart, Sean muscled the steering wheel, hanging a U and pulling into his own driveway across the street. Not even bothering to take his books, he jumped down and ran in the front door.

"SEAN, IS THAT YOU?" his mother yelled when he walked in. She was vacuuming in the dining room, and Max, a neighbor's kid, was on the floor playing with one of Sean's robots. The house smelled like spaghetti sauce.

"YEAH, MOM, I'M HOME." He ran up the stairs, taking four at a time. It was just as noisy up there. His mom had one of her jazz records on his stereo louder than he played the Talking Heads. He could hear her singing along with it through the floor.

He slipped into his parents' bedroom and sat on the big bed, placing the phone in his lap. His heart started that scary skipping again, and he took a deep breath. He'd memorized Brooke's number, even though he'd never called her — just like he knew her address, her locker number, and the license plates of the funny old Rambler she drove to school.

But before he started to dial he heard a ring and felt a shaking in his hands, and for a second he wasn't sure what was going on. He stared at the phone as if he'd never heard one ring before, as if it were alive. Then he collapsed with disappointment. It was probably Nick or Meg or his father calling before leaving the bicycle store. Now he'd have to go through this whole thing to get his nerve up to call again.

He picked up the receiver at the same time as his mother downstairs. The vacuuming stopped.

"Hello," she said.

"Hi. Can I speak to Sean, please?"

Sean clutched the phone, cradled it against his face, and threw himself back on the bed. It was

Brooke. BROOKE!! *She* was calling *him*. He panicked and sat up again. Sure it sounded like her, but it could be his imagination. Since Monday he kept seeing her in the halls, the cafeteria, the parking lot, only to run over and find out it was really someone else. Maybe this was only Allie or some girl who wanted math tutoring.

"Sure. Who's calling, please?"

"This is Brooke Applebaum."

"SEAN, IT'S BROOOOKKKKE APPPLLLE-BAAUUM!" His mother screamed, and Sean mouthed ecstatically at the same time.

"I'VE GOT IT, MOM!" His voice did a tiny slide, something that hadn't happened to him since he was fourteen. He tried to calm himself and put the phone to his ear.

"Hi, Brooke," he said. Supercool.

"Hi, Sean."

Neither of them said anything but there was so much noise. His mom had started the vacuum again and on Brooke's end he heard kids screaming, a dog barking, and somebody singing along with an opera record.

"Hi."

"I just wanted to say hi," she explained. He could barely hear her. "Um, since I haven't seen you all week. I wanted to know if you were mad at me because I got your friend Allie in trouble."

"No. Oh, no. Not at all." He'd finally asked Allie what had happened on the field trip. Unlike Celia and her friends, Allie insisted that Brooke was totally blameless. Sean pressed the receiver to his ear. He didn't want to miss a word.

"Good," she said. "Well, that's all, I guess. I

thought you saw me yesterday outside the gym and you didn't come over and say hello so. . . ."

"No, I didn't see you," Sean lied. That was the one time he had succeeded in finding her, but he was with Celia and the whole crowd so he couldn't make himself go over.

"Oh. I thought you did."

"Brooke, hold on for a sec." Sean ran into the hall. "MOM, CAN YOU TURN THAT OFF!" He ducked into his room and turned down the stereo. He threw himself on the bed in his parents' room. "I'm back. It was kind of noisy."

"That's better."

"Yeah."

He couldn't stand it anymore. Trying to make small talk over the phone was torture, and besides, what he really wanted was to see her, to be with her. "Listen, Brooke, do you want to get together Saturday night? I'm not sure what we'll do or anything, but I want to see you and I know I should have called earlier but I still think we'd have a great time. So do you think you might want to?"

It was taking forever for her to answer, even though Sean knew it was only a few seconds.

"Okay."

"Okay? You mean, yes? Really?"

"Sure."

"Great. I'll pick you up at seven-thirty. I know where you live."

"See you on Saturday."

He put the phone down as if it were something rare and precious and floated back onto the bed, hugging a pillow and staring out the window. A tiny breeze rumpled the curtains, giving him a glimpse of Celia storming out her front door and stomping over to Meg's.

He watched her, his anger and frustration completely gone. He didn't want to think about Celia anymore or about Nick or Darcy or any of it. The only thing he could think about was how in the world he was going to make it until seven-thirty on Saturday.

CHAPTER 7

Allie couldn't find it.

She'd been across the quad twice, by the library and the main office, past the greenhouse, and the industrial arts center. She was all the way over to the gym when she realized that it was almost fifteen minutes after the final bell. If she couldn't find the drama studio soon, she might as well give up.

It was sunny. Beach weather. Girls in track shorts jogged by, as did boys suited up for baseball and a couple of PE teachers. She was really starting to sweat under her heavy wool sweater and long skirt. "Where is this stupid building?" she muttered to herself.

The drama studio had been built that fall, when she was away. The lowliest freshman would be able to direct her to it. But she couldn't get herself to walk up to anyone and say the words. The decision to try out for the play was too risky, too important, too private to share with a stranger.

"Oh, no." She was heading back across the parking lot when she spotted Celia and Meg leaning against the hood of Maria Martinez's station wagon, surrounded by four other girls. All of them had their faces tipped to the sun, beginning their 1987 tans. Allie prayed that they wouldn't see her. If she couldn't admit to a stranger where she was going, she certainly wouldn't be able to tell her old friends. She put her head down and skirted back toward campus, sticking close to the fence and moving fast.

"ALLIE!!! HEY, ALLIE!!!!"

Caught. Allie's stomach dropped like a sharp rock. She'd spent three days talking herself into going to this audition, and now her ambition was getting scared and ready to run.

Celia and Meg were waving. After a moment the other girls waved, too. Allie froze while Celia, in a pink sundress, and Meg, in jeans and a red polo shirt, ran over to meet her.

"We're all going to Bruno's downtown to do some more planning for College Day," said Meg. "You want to come?"

Bruno's was a hip café in back of a huge bookstore. Allie used to go there with L.P. The memory hit her like a slap in the face.

"I can't."

"Why not?" Celia asked with a tinge of annoyance. She'd been getting more and more annoyed since Allie'd begun to refuse her invitations: No, Celia, I will not go bowling with you and your friends on Saturday night. No, I don't want your mother to redye my hair at her beauty shop.

81

No, I won't go to the next junior class meeting.
Why didn't they understand how much better it
was if she said no.

Allie slung her bag over her shoulder and
walked backward. "Because, I have to, um, to go
to the library. To study."

Celia and Meg exchanged glances. Allie never
used to study much, and she could tell they didn't
know whether to believe her and take it as a sign
that she was reforming, or accuse of her handing
them an out-and-out lie.

But Allie didn't give them a chance to figure it
out. She bolted, waving, and not looking back.
Even though she didn't know where she was
going, she knew if she took one more second to
doubt . . . or think . . . or feel . . . she was lost. It
was enough just fighting the memories that
pricked her as she crossed the campus again. The
auditorium where she'd had her first orientation.
The table in the cafeteria where she used to meet
her friends and L.P. Thorson's computer center,
the rose bushes, and the fragrant grass. Ms.
Pittman's photo room and the sculpture garden
that used to have only one piece of sculpture
in it.

Allie stopped by the art rooms, surrounded by
abstract metal art pieces and hunks of molded
clay. Right in front of her a door was open and
voices were spilling out. She remembered it as
the art workshop, but now it had a sign on the
door that said DRAMA STUDIO. AUDITIONS TODAY
FOR *Our Town*.

Excitement and relief mixed with fear. Slowly,
Allie peeked in. She didn't see anyone so she

stepped into the foyer. There was a curved wall covered with posters and old programs, photographs, and schedules. It still smelled of paint and wet clay. There was an opening to one side and Allie walked over to peek in.

She took a few steps up and there it was, a cozy little theater — a platform backed by dark drapes and surrounded on three sides by about five rows of seats. The theater was so small that more than half the seats were filled with auditioners. And as much as Meg and Celia's friends looked alike, that's how much some of these kids looked different. There was a fat girl talking to a jock, a beauty joking with a boy who wore eye makeup, some very straight-looking kids, and a few that made her look like a cheerleader.

And in the middle of it all was Brooke, in a pair of lavender overalls, with a pencil behind her ear and a tape measure draped through her hammer loop. She was talking to Ms. Smith, the drama teacher, but popped up as soon as she saw Allie and ran over.

"Hi! You came. Everybody already signed up but I'll just write you in." Brooke pulled a Xeroxed paper off of her clipboard. "This is what you're supposed to read. It's a scene between Mrs. Gibbs and Emily."

"Thanks."

Brooke led her in and they sat down together in the back row. Kids turned around to stare, but they merely looked curious. Once they took her in, they smiled and went back to what they were doing.

Brooke leaned in. "Old Weaver didn't call you into the office or anything, did she?"

"No. She spared me that."

"I'm so sorry you got in trouble. It was all my fault."

"No," Allie insisted. "Besides, it was worth it."

Brooke tapped her arm and stood up. "I have to go help Ms. Smith. I'll talk to you later. Good luck."

Allie slunk down in her seat as Ms. Smith called pairs of students up to read from the Xeroxed pages. She tried to look over her lines and figure out what she would do when she got up there. They were only reading two pages, so Allie had lots of time to read it quietly to herself and go over and over it in her head. Still, when her name was called, she felt jangly and unprepared.

She walked down the aisle and onto the stage. Her legs were wobbly and she could feel a trickle of sweat zip down her back.

"Allie, have you ever been in a play before?" asked Ms. Smith. She was young, with very curly hair and intense eyes.

"No," Allie answered in a small voice. Still, she was glad that any voice had come out at all.

Ms. Smith didn't say anything for a moment and looked at her notes instead. "But I did readings out loud at another school and I'm really interested," Allie suddenly blurted.

The teacher looked up slowly and smiled. Allie decided it was an okay smile, one you could trust. "All right," Ms. Smith told her, "why don't you read Mrs. Gibbs and Stacy will read Emily."

Stacy was a frail-looking sophomore who'd been called before her. She was standing to one side of the stage and came forward when Ms. Smith said her name. The two girls looked at each other for a moment, but neither one of them could smile. Finally Ms. Smith motioned with a pencil. "Begin, please."

Allie read the first words. They came out louder and clearer than she thought they would. The way she felt, she'd worried that her tongue would be stuck like glue but no . . . Stacy seemed to understand what she was reading, and when Allie finished, she followed with her line from the script. Then it was Allie's turn again. Her voice rose and she kept going. Then Stacy read back, only this time it wasn't so much like Stacy . . . this time it was more like the character in the play. Allie read her next line and decided this was a little bit like tennis, only tennis where you played with your guts and your emotions. Allie began to relax. She felt safer up on the stage than she had anywhere else in Redwood High.

Finally they came to the end. They were standing closer now, and when they were done there was a silence that neither girl could break.

"Good," Ms. Smith told them.

Allie wasn't sure how to react. She started to step down.

"Stay up there, Allie. I'd like you two to switch roles."

Allie nodded, looking up. But at that moment something caught her eye that scared her confidence away. First she saw his camera, then his dark hair and angular face. Standing in the aisle, wearing an Army surplus jacket and a baseball cap, was L.P! He was looking down, loading his camera. What was he doing there? Allie looked up again and saw the *Guardian* sticker on his bag. Of course. He was photographing the auditions for the school paper. Her knees began to shake but she stayed put, not sure if he'd seen her or not.

She heard Stacy's voice begin, and she was about to say her line when she couldn't resist looking up again, just a glance. When she did, she wished she hadn't. A girl, a pretty girl, ducked under L.P.'s arms and playfully took his camera from him. He kept his arms around her, pressing his cheek to hers as he showed her where to point it and what to press.

A bright light exploded and Allie felt like the explosion was inside her own heart. For a moment she couldn't see and then she heard Ms. Smith and Brooke yelling at the girl for taking a flash picture, but she only heard part of it because the rest of the sound was her hard boots thudding on the carpet and then the grass, and then smacking shiny linoleum. She ran, weaving around a janitor with his cart and a couple of seniors flirting by an open locker. She heard other footsteps behind her, but they didn't matter until she heard L.P.'s voice.

"Al! Allie!" L.P. was coming after her, holding something dark against his chest. "Wait up. You left your purse."

She didn't want to stop and see him but she'd come to the dead end of the hallway. There was nowhere else to go. She faced the lockers and the classroom doors and wished she could kick through them with her foot. Quickly she turned around, stole her bag out of his hands, and tried to make it past him.

He grabbed her arm. "Al, I'm sorry the flash went off, but you don't have to freak out. Betsy's just a beginner. I'm showing her the ropes. She didn't know she wasn't supposed to take a flash picture while somebody was up onstage."

"Well, I'm sure you'll teach her," Allie said as nastily as possible. Her tears were starting to pour. "Why didn't you just kiss her while you were showing her how to take a picture? It was all for my benefit, wasn't it?"

L.P. let her go. He glared at her. There was a new sadness in his eyes, one that she didn't remember from their two years together. "What is this?" he said, shaking his head. "Jealousy! Isn't it a little late for that? You're the one that broke up with me, remember? You're the one who wouldn't even give me an explanation, Allie. How do you think that made me feel? Why shouldn't I be dating somebody else now? For all I know, you had some hot love affair in New York."

That almost made Allie scream. A love affair! She barely had a friend in New York, let alone a love affair. She pushed him away and ran down the aisle. Allie broke the doors open that led outside. This time, L.P. didn't follow. By the time she'd run another fifty yards, her chest was heaving and her skin was hot.

She was alone now, she decided, as alone as she had been in New York City. It wasn't place that was the problem; it wasn't even her old friends. It was her . . . Allie. She'd changed and she'd never be the same. Worse, she couldn't find anything to fill up the emptiness. She'd tried. For a moment back there in the theater it had felt like it might work. But now that was gone, too.

She walked slowly to the front of the school, and when she got there, she headed for the street and the long way home. The late afternoon sun beat down on her but she didn't feel hot or sweaty, or anything. She just kept walking, slowly, aimlessly, and — for the first time since she'd come back — really without hope.

CHAPTER 8

RRRRRRRRRRKKKKKKKKKK!

The floor glistened. The bowling ball, all blue and marbled, wobbled and bounced down the lane. It hesitated, it curved, it made a vibration that Meg could feel through the bottom of her feet. And then, as usual, it hopped into the gutter.

"GUTTER BALL!! GUTTER BALL!!!" everybody chanted, over and over.

Meg put her hands over her face and pummeled the floor with her feet. "Oh, no, not a gutter ball again," she cried. She turned to her team, juniors, seniors, and sophomores sitting in and on top of a turquoise plastic booth, all wearing headbands that said AARDVARKS. She fell to her knees in disgrace. "I let you down again, fellow Aardvarks. And I'm your captain. Can you ever forgive me?"

Patrick, who had made the Aardvark head-bands, pulled his down over his eyes and crossed his arms. Other team members pretended to cry. Some fell over the bench and moaned. Celia picked up an empty Coke can and tipped it over her head.

It was part of the ritual. They called it Bowling for Dollars or Dodos Go Bowling. It had started last fall when they were hanging out one Saturday and ended up at Ray's Lanes because they had nothing better to do. They'd decided to bowl and discovered that there was something silly, undignified, and absurd about the whole game. It became a great way to goof around and blow off steam. And that was exactly what Meg needed. After the last two weeks, she didn't want to think about College Day or midterms or the problems of her friends. She was relieved that neither Sean nor Allie was there. She needed an evening where she could just have a good time.

Nick came up next. His team wore sleeveless men's undershirts that said WOMBATS. Nick had his over a rugby shirt and it came down almost to his knees.

"Make room for the master," he teased. He aimed. He spun around three times. He made a face, pretended to spit on the ball, and threw.

A strike!

"OOOOOOO," everyone roared.

"Non gutter ball!" cheered Sam Pond.

"Nick, you're not supposed to do that," Meg teased, staring down the lane.

Nick was more amazed than she was. He turned to her and grinned. "Sometimes I just can't help it."

Meg laughed. It felt so good to really let go.

When Nick's bowling ball popped back he picked it up and started to make little squealy noises as he pushed it toward her. Suddenly his handsome face looked about ten years old and they were right back in middle school. "Hey. McCall," he said, "what's this?"

"I don't know and I don't want to find out."

Nick lowered the ball, a sly smile passing over his face. "It's the creature from *Aliens*, you know. the one that came out of the guy's stomach." Nick quickly tugged out his rugby shirt and his Wombat T-shirt and pushed the bowling ball underneath. Then he started acting as if he had the hiccups, like the people in the movie. Finally the ball emerged from under his shirt, along with more squealy sounds.

Meg howled. "Gross."

"Nick is losing it," yelled Celia.

Nick put the ball back on the rack and came after Meg again, this time with his hands raised as if he were Dracula. She figured that he must have been ready for a blow-out himself, which made sense since he always seemed to be on such good behavior with his girl friends.

"Nick!!"

He swept his arms around her and began nibbling at the base of her neck, inside the collar of her blouse. Meg threw her head back. She couldn't stop laughing. She flashed on the laughing jags Allie used to go on when they were younger and understood now how it was that Allie couldn't stop. Nick kept laughing, too, and nibbling, and holding her tight around the waist.

"WOULD YOU GUYS STOP IT!"

Nick's arms went slack. He turned around with a questioning look on his face.

It was Darcy. She was in beige jodhpurs, a frilly blouse, camel tweed vest, and scuffed red and green bowling shoes. It was her first experience with Dodos Go Bowling and Meg had a feeling she was not the goof-around-and-get-silly type. For starters, she'd refused to wear her Wombat T-shirt.

Darcy put on a forced smile. "I just mean, if we're going to play, let's play, not stand here watching the two of you act stupid."

"Oh, Darce," Nick teased, turning his back to Meg, "are we stupid? Are you embarrassed to be seen with us in front of all the important people at this bowling alley?"

Darcy narrowed her eyes and folded her arms. She moved close to him. "People are staring at you."

Nick looked down the lanes. A few other bowlers were watching. There were two fat men in the next lane chugging a six-pack, and a Boy Scout troop on the other side. Nick pointed to the Boy Scouts. "I don't know, Darce. They're probably spies from Bradley College, scouting out new students."

Darcy hit his chest. "Oh, Nick."

He grabbed her. "And now that they've seen you here with stupid me, it's all over. They're not going to let you in now." He grinned and tickled her until she stopped hitting and started giggling. Then she wrapped her hands around his neck and started kissing him right in the middle of the lane.

Meg was still standing on the other side of Nick. Suddenly her giddy mood had turned dull. "Hey, you guys, talk about attracting attention." Darcy stopped kissing Nick, but kept her arms around his neck.

Nick chucked Darcy under the chin and took one of her hands. "Come on, Darce. You go next for our team."

Now Darcy was all softness and smiles. "Okay." She let Nick lead her back to the table where Sam was keeping score.

As soon as Meg realized that she was staring at Nick and Darcy, she turned to her own team and yelled, "Who's next for us? Come on, Cici." She pulled Celia up and pushed her onto the lane. Then Meg floundered for a moment, not sure quite what to do with herself. Looking to pump her spirits back up, she noticed Patrick. He was watching her, smiling, sitting on the end of the bench in jeans and a worn denim shirt. She plopped down on his lap.

"Hi, fellow Aardvark." She pulled his headband down around his neck.

"Hi," Patrick said back, sitting up a little straighter. His sweet eyes got very wide.

Meg slung her arm around him. His shirt was soft as a baby's blanket. Meg leaned her cheek against his shoulder.

Patrick didn't move a muscle.

"I failed my teammates," Meg sighed.

"Nah," Patrick said with a funny laugh. He cleared his throat. "You could never fail anybody."

Meg took his can of soda and sipped it. Celia

was curtsying after knocking down five pins, and then two more. "Thattaway, Cici!" Meg cheered, lifting her head. She watched Darcy take off her vest and hand it to Nick before getting up to bowl.

"If Darcy gets an eight or better, the Wombats win it," Sam announced, holding up his score sheet.

All eyes went to the line where Darcy was leaning over, tossing her hair, and trying to figure out how to hold the ball. She looked back at Nick, who gave her a little wave, motioning her to go ahead. Darcy broke into a huge smile, swung her arm, staggered a few steps back from the weight, and let go of the ball. It rolled out of her hand, hit the floor with a blop, and then only went two or three feet more before it stopped, dead center in the middle of the lane.

Meg's team went wild. Meg yelled, "Darcy, don't you know you're supposed to roll the ball, not drop it!" She leaned back against Patrick again and laughed.

"Yeah," Patrick added, "you're not supposed to dump it on the middle of the lane. An Aardvark would never do that."

Darcy stomped back to the bench and took off her bowling shoes, throwing them on the floor. She pulled on her vest so furiously that she buttoned it up wrong and didn't even notice. Nick crept onto the lane to pick up her bowling ball. After he put it back on the rack, Darcy stormed over to him.

She wrapped herself around him and dug her

face into his shoulder. "Nick, this is a stupid game. I don't want to play anymore. Let's go get something to eat. I'm hungry."

Nick looked over at Meg, who was still perched on Patrick's lap. Maria Martinez was throwing the last ball for the Aardvarks. There was a crash and a cheer as she knocked down eight pins.

"Usually we all hang out in the coffee shop upstairs, Darce," Nick said. "We can go up there if you want to."

She looked like a little girl who was being forced to eat something she hated. "Yuck. Let's go somewhere decent. I hate this place. Let's go to the Bubble."

Meg hopped to her feet as Maria threw the final ball, knocking down one pin and winning it for the Aardvarks. She took both of Patrick's warm hands and pulled him up next to her. He leaped up as if he were on springs. "Yeah, Patrick, why don't we go to the Bubble Café, too." She wasn't sure why she said it. The words had just flown out. "You have your car, don't you?" She nudged his stomach, which was lean and hard. "We can celebrate our win."

Patrick stared at her, his eyes getting wider and wider. "Sure!"

Darcy glared at Meg and led the way out. She walked as fast as she could, even though she was just in her knee socks and her feet kept skating and sliding. She finally made it to the rental booth and handed in her bowling shoes, which were too small and smelled bad. When she saw her black riding boots come back over the counter she almost cried. She hugged them to her chest, before tugging them on and hurrying out to the parking lot.

Darcy pushed open the front door and was hit by damp, cool air. What a relief. Finally she was away from that rumbly echo, and those scary looking pin machines, and the smell of greasy burgers. Most of all she was glad to get away from Nick's stupid friends! Why in the world did they think that was fun? Fun was watching movies and skiing and partying — stuff where you could look good and make an impression and have people to impress. But tonight she got the feeling that the only person Nick was interested in impressing was Meg McCall.

Darcy pulled open the door to Nick's Rabbit and climbed in, her breath making little clouds. Nick would be out here soon, she knew he would follow her. He was too polite and well-brought-up not to.

Sure enough, Nick rapped on the glass. She pushed his door open, but he stayed in the doorway. "Darcy, those are my friends," he accused. Darcy slid down in the seat. He was angry. "Why did you have to run off like that? What's your problem?"

"I'm hungry. It's after seven."

"Come on, Darcy. You just got uptight because they laughed at you. Can't you take a joke? It's all in fun."

Darcy made her voice sound as if she was on the edge of tears. "Maybe to you it's fun. Being laughed at is not my idea of a great time."

Nick got in and slammed the door.

"Nick," Darcy moved closer. "Why don't we go somewhere?"

"Where," Nick interrupted nastily, "to Marci's?"

"No." The last time they'd partied at Marci's Nick had been the one to walk out, saying he was bored. "Just the two of us. We always have a good time alone. Things just get weird when we're around other people."

"Well, there are other people in the world, Darcy. Besides, I like being with my friends."

Darcy knew one weapon she had that Nick's "friends" could not compete with. This was the one area where being a year older and more experienced sure helped. She inched even closer and ran her fingertips up his arm. "I'm sorry, Nick. I just wasn't having a good time."

"Well, I was."

It was a challenge now, to get control, and Darcy knew she could succeed. She tugged at the collar of his polo shirt and started kissing him softly up the side of his neck.

"Cut it out, Darce."

She didn't stop. She put a hand in his hair and whispered. "Let's not go to the café. Let's go park. Okay?"

He didn't say anything, but she could see his hands relax around the steering wheel. She kept kissing. Finally he grabbed her shoulder and pulled her in. He had that fuzzy look on his face that told her she was going to win.

But just then there was a knock on the glass.

Nick tensed up again and let her go. Furious, Darcy folded her arms and sat up.

Nick waited a second, caught his breath, then cranked open his window. Patrick Delancie was standing outside, making crunching noises as he stomped the gravel with his cowboy boots. Meg stood behind Patrick. She leaned on the open door of Patrick's rusty old sedan.

"Sorry to bug you guys, but my car's totally dead," Patrick explained. "It might be the battery. Do you have any jumper cables?"

"I don't. Sorry." Nick looked past Patrick at Meg.

Nick started for his door to get out and help, but Darcy grabbed his arm and leaned across him. "I'm sure someone inside has some," Darcy insisted quickly. Patrick had an ancient car that smelled from all the stray animals he picked up. It figured that it wouldn't even start. "Go in and ask."

Patrick and Meg started back into the bowling alley. Nick leaned out the window and yelled, "Why don't you two come with us. You can come back tomorrow and get your car."

"Nick!" Darcy objected under her breath.

He pretended he didn't hear her.

Patrick asked Meg, "Is that okay with you?"

Meg hesitated, peering in at Nick and Darcy. Then she smiled, flung back her long hair, and laced her arm through Patrick's. "Sure."

"Great," Darcy grumbled under her breath as Meg and Patrick climbed into the backseat. Patrick seemed happy as anything and Meg was in a fine mood, and now even Nick seemed cheery and relaxed. Well, that was just hunky-dory. Let them all think this was a great idea. As far as Darcy was concerned, she'd make this an evening they'd never forget.

CHAPTER 9

"Hey, Brooke. . . . Nah, sounds too cool. Whoooo, Applebaum. . . . Too phony. So, what do you want to do? . . . That sounds dumb, like I don't know where to take her. Yeah, Brooke, so let's hurry it up, the new *Star Trek* movie starts at eight. . . . Ugh, that sounds like I'm a jerk and I don't care what she wants to do. How about, look Applebaum, let's drive around for a while and see how we feel. . . . Forget it, that sounds like I can't wait to jump her bones."

Sean eased his parents' van up the small hill that led to Brooke's house. The motor sounded like machine-gun fire and the inside reeked of Lysol and Windex. He'd spent half the day cleaning it, trying to get rid of the grease and rubber smell from all those bicycles. Now it reminded him of the dressing room for the public pool.

His van continued to chug as he looked for the number. Brooke didn't live in the country, near the vineyards and the ranches, like Nick and Allie. And she didn't live near downtown, like he, Meg and Celia. She lived sort of in between, in one of these older houses with clotheslines and big lawns, garden plots and small pens for rabbits or chickens. Sean squinted at the curb numbers. He was getting closer. And more nervous.

The whole prospect of dating made Sean want to spend the rest of his life with his robots and his computer. So far he'd only asked out two freshmen, and they were both so dippy and intimidated that it didn't matter. He'd taken one to a rock concert and the other bowling with his friends, and neither date had been much fun. Of course, he never felt about them the way he felt about Brooke.

The numbers on the houses were getting higher. Pretty soon he saw it — Brooke's address. It was another older clapboard house, one with window boxes and a swing made out of an old rubber tire hanging from the front tree. It looked tall enough to be three stories. Sean tried to stay cool.

After he parked the van, he pulled down the visor to examine the spot where he'd nicked his chin shaving. He smoothed his hair. He checked his breath by blowing into his hand. He got out and retucked his gas station shirt. When he walked to the door, he was still trying to decide what he should say. . . . Hello, what's happening? . . . Hey, you look great. . . . So what's new? . . . He didn't want to sound too casual, but

he didn't want to sound like this was the most
important night of his life, either. He got to the
porch, went up the steps, and made himself ring.
A minute later he heard thumps leading to the
door. He braced himself. It swung open.

"Um. . . ."

Sean didn't get a word out. A girl, younger
than Brooke by about five years and with thick,
thick glasses was staring at him. Next to her a
huge sheep dog had both paws on the front screen
door and was barking as though Sean were a
burglar. Inside there was loud opera music coming over a stereo. But even louder than that was
what came out of the girl's mouth next. She
turned and sang, "BROOKE, YOUR BOY-
FRIEND'S HERE!"

"HE'S NOT MY BOYFRIEND!"

"WELL, HE'S A BOY AND HE'S YOUR
FRIEND AND HE'S. . . ."

"OKAY, OKAY! I'LL BE RIGHT DOWN."

"Come on in," the girl told him, swinging back
the door and holding onto the dog's collar.

Sean watched the dog and squeezed through.
Fortunately, the dog just took a couple of sniffs
and then trotted off. The girl stayed. "I'm Corin.
Brooke's sister," she told him. "Brooke said you
were coming. We're all going to a concert at the
college. Except Brooke. She was supposed to go,
and she and my dad got in a fight because she
wanted to go out with you instead, but my mom
said she didn't have to go to the concert if she
didn't — "

"Corin!" a familiar voice threatened. It was
Brooke. She stood on the bottom stair with one

hand on the rail. She wore overalls with a lacy T-shirt underneath. Her curls were a little damp over her forehead and her cheeks were bright pink, as if she'd just come from a hot shower. Sean stared and stared. He tried to remember if he'd decided on his first words or not.

"Hi."

"Hi."

"My sister talks a lot."

"Brooke, everybody in our family talks a lot."

Brooke glared at her little sister, who wrinkled her nose and walked off. Sean stared some more. Finally Brooke walked over to him.

"I hope this is okay," she said, referring to her overalls and not quite looking at him. "I didn't know where we were going, and I figured I'd probably just wear the wrong thing anyway, so I decided this was the most comfortable."

Sean was so glad to see her again. "Sure. Where do you want to go?"

"Oh, I don't know. Where do you want to go?"

"I don't know. Where do you want to go?"

"Well, uh, I don't know. Where do you think we should go?" Suddenly Brooke laughed and covered her face with her hands. When she lifted it again she smiled in this wonderful way that let Sean know that she was nervous, too . . . and that it didn't matter. "I guess neither of us knows."

"No. I guess not."

She took his hand and led him into the living room.

The Applebaum living room had wood beams across the ceiling and an old-fashioned chandelier. There was stuff everywhere: open books, dog toys, a butterfly net, an ant farm, and for some reason, a clock attached to a potato. A big stereo was playing the opera music that he'd heard at the door, and Brooke turned it down before sitting next to him on an old-fashioned velvet sofa. "Everybody'll be leaving in a few minutes. If you want, we can check the newspaper and figure out what there is to do."

"Okay." Actually, now that Sean thought about it, just sitting in that living room with Brooke sounded better than anything else he could imagine.

Just then, the sound of about ten different kinds of shoes came clomping down the stairs, and then five people and the sheep dog stood at the bottom. Sean rocketed up to meet them.

"Sean, these are my folks and my sister Daphne and my other sister Ainsley. You already met Corin."

"Hi."

"Hello, Sean."

"Hi."

They stood in a line. All the sisters were younger than Brooke and a little bit goofy-looking. Mr. Applebaum, who was wearing a fisherman's hat and a tweed jacket, checked his watch. "We've got to get going." He looked at Brooke. "Sure you two don't want to come with us?"

"I'm sure, Dad."

Mr. Applebaum leaned in to shake Sean's hand. "You'll have her home by eleven-thirty?"

"Yes, sir."

Her father smiled.

"Let's go," urged Brooke's mom, who was freckled and blonde and pretty. She looked a lot like Brooke. "Have a good time." She pulled Brooke's father out and the whole gang of them, except the dog, followed. Each sister waved and then the door closed behind them.

Sean stood staring after them for a while. "Your sisters have kind of unusual names."

Brooke grinned. "I know."

They stood there in the middle of the front hall, gazing at each other again. Sean couldn't quite get himself to move, and he was glad when she led the way back to the living room sofa. She opened the *Redwood Hills Daily* and set it between them.

They sat quietly and looked at the movie listings. It seemed kind of odd to be in this room . . . just the two of them, reading the paper, surrounded by the ant farm and all the other junk. Sean slid a little closer to Brooke.

"I missed you all week," he heard himself say. He was a little scared after he said it, but then Brooke's face lit up. Her eyes got big and bright and her cheeks went even pinker. He wanted her to always look exactly like that.

"I missed you, too."

Sean rested his arm on the back of the sofa, hoping to let it drop naturally around her shoulder. She smelled of baby powder and shampoo. He was feeling incredibly warm inside, almost light-headed as he inched closer, his arm touching those wispy curls at the back of her neck.

He was working up the nerve to kiss her again when suddenly something sharp bit into the back of his leg. He jumped up.

"OUCH!"

"What's wrong?"

"OW! OOH! I think something bit me." Sean hopped and rubbed behind his knee. Then he saw it, a furry purplish bug was sticking to the back of his trousers, hanging on. Sean tried batting it off but it didn't budge. It was really big. "What is it?" he panicked.

Brooke fell back on the sofa and started to laugh.

"What's funny?"

"I'm sorry. It's just. . . ."

"What?"

"Hold still, I'll get it off."

"It's huge!"

"I know. It's okay," she wheezed, still laughing. "Don't worry. It's not a real bug." Sean looked over his shoulder as she unhooked the bug from the back of his leg. She pulled him down next to her again and handed the bug to him. It was some kind of homemade fly imitation attached to a fishhook. Brooke kept laughing, and Sean started to feel self-conscious and dumb. He knew that Brooke wasn't really laughing at him, but he hated it nonetheless. He'd been made fun of too many times in his life to take it lightly.

"My dad uses it when he goes fishing," Brooke explained, still giggling. "To catch fish." She held it in her palm and showed him. "It's called a fly. He always leaves them around. I kind of like them."

106

"You do?"

"Sure. I used to collect bugs when I was little. My dad would take me fishing with him, and we'd study the bugs in the water — see what the fish were eating. Maybe it's because he just has daughters or something, but he always said we should be interested in everything, not just what's supposed to be for girls."

"You never thought that was weird, to be interested in fish?"

Brooke shrugged.

Sean's self-consciousness started to ease. He thought of Brooke at school with her hammer hanging from her overalls, and how other kids thought she was so strange. He slowly sat back down. "Don't you ever worry about what people think, though? I mean, if they tease you or think it's bizarre that you like bugs?"

"Or build sets or wear the wrong thing or be the only person in class to do a report on getting energy out of a potato?"

Sean glanced over at the clock — so that's why it was wired into a potato! The potato was decomposing and providing power to run the clock.

Brooke's face grew very serious. She set the fishing fly on the end table. "I used to. I know that some kids laugh at me, and for about a year — I guess it was in eighth grade or so — I tried really hard to be like everybody else. And you know what?"

"What?"

"They still laughed at me, and it was much worse because I wasn't doing any of the things I like to do. And I guess I realized I'm not like everybody else, and that's okay. I have good friends and I get to do interesting stuff and now I think it's really important to be who you are and not worry about what other people think. But I guess you wouldn't know so much about that. You're so popular and all."

"Me?" Sean gasped in a high voice.

"Sure. Your crowd is the popular crowd in the school."

"And I'm the weirdest one in that crowd."

"Just because you're smart. . . ."

"Brooke, you didn't know me when I was a freshman."

"What does that have to do with it?"

"I was the original geek! I weighed about eighty pounds and the older guys picked on me like crazy. My first month of high school I got taped to the flagpole. Taped!" Sean's hands started to shake. He couldn't quite believe he was telling her this — he never talked about it anymore, not even to Nick, who'd been the one to cut him free. "Sophomore year stuff like that happened, too," he said, fighting back the memories.

"So what?" Brooke argued. "We're juniors now. After next year we'll be out of high school, and it'll be a lot more important to be smart like you are or to know how to build something or catch a fish, than to just know how to be like everybody else so you won't get laughed at!"

Sean suddenly knew she was right and threw his arms around her. He held her hard, burying his face against her shoulder. She hugged him back as bravely as she embraced the rest of the world, pressing against him in a way that made him feel that nothing could ever get between them. Her hair was soft and slightly damp, and there was that baby powder smell and the warmth and strength of her slim body against his. He slid his hand along the side of her face and when she looked at him again, he kissed her. He didn't think about it. It just happened, the most natural thing in the world. His mouth against hers. Long, slow, and gentle. It was better than the first time because he wasn't just kissing her because he liked the way she looked. He was attracted to who she really was inside.

When they let go of each other they were both flushed and breathless. They smiled. Sean took her hand. Finally, he pointed to the newspaper again and said, "So, do you still want to go out? Not that I'd mind just staying here. But if your parents came back and found us I have a feeling they might have a few things to say."

"Not to mention my sisters."

Sean laughed. He brushed a stray curl from her forehead. "So, we're back to where we started, I guess. Where should we go?"

"I really don't care," Brooke answered, gazing up at him, "as long as it's with you."

Sean suddenly felt ambitious, almost reckless. "My friends are probably still at the bowling alley. We could go hang out with them."

Brooke sat tall. "Okay."

Sean hugged her again. She made him feel brave enough to tackle anything.

CHAPTER 10

The Bubble Café turned out to be a bust.

Nick and Darcy and Meg and Patrick sat at a booth across from each other while the waitresses ran back and forth in their pink outfits, rows of dishes stacked up and down their arms. The food smelled good, especially the onion rings; the music was loud and tight; the chatter in the place was typically Saturday-night happy; but Meg had lost her appetite. She had to sit there with Patrick while Darcy kissed Nick, tickled him, sat on his lap, made little private giggles, and whispered into his ear. By the time the milk shakes and the burgers arrived, practically everybody in the café was staring at them. And poor Patrick — every time he saw Nick and Darcy giggling or smooching he turned beet red and looked as if he wanted to crawl under the table.

So Meg was relieved to finally be heading home. Nick and Darcy were entwined in the front seat — Meg kept wondering if Nick could drive safely — while she and Patrick sat self-consciously in the back. The car stereo was playing a slow song.

They were heading into Meg's neighborhood when Darcy snuggled and sighed, "Let's go to the top of Capitola Mountain and look at the lights." She turned around as if she'd just remembered that there were other people in the car. Her hair was mussed and even her dimples looked hazy. "You two don't mind, do you?"

Meg didn't know what to say. The top of Capitola was the most notorious parking spot in all of Redwood Hills. What was she supposed to do up there? Sit and watch Nick and Darcy make out? But it seemed harsh and prudish for her to demand to go home, or refuse to drive up there. She didn't say anything.

Patrick cleared his throat. He glanced briefly at Meg as they turned onto Capitola Mountain Drive. With the first steep curve he was thrown against Meg. "Sorry," he whispered.

"That's okay."

They were climbing the hills, the trees and lights spreading out below them, heading to the spot where you could see over the whole town. When they got there, three or four other cars were parked. They pulled up into a secluded spot and Nick turned off the lights.

Meg felt like ice inside. Nick and Darcy started necking right away. Meg thought of getting out of the car, but finally turned to look at Patrick. He was staring at her.

When Meg met Patrick's eyes, he looked down

shyly. The moonlight cast a shadow across his face, which looked sensitive and handsome. Patrick tentatively reached across the seat and took her hand. His palm was dry and warm, and he just sat there very still for a second, as if he was working up his nerve, or deciding what to do.

Finally he reached for her shoulder and pulled her toward him. Even though his eyes were closed, Meg could see the emotion in his face as he leaned in. But what amazed her most was the way she felt inside when he kissed her. The ice melted away. And so did Darcy and Nick.

Patrick leaned his forehead on her shoulder and laughed, a sweet, soft laugh. Meg liked his long hair against her face, the soft denim of his shirt, and the way she could feel his heart pounding underneath.

"Boy, have I been wanting to do that for a long time," Patrick said, heaving a sigh.

Meg started to laugh softly, too, a warm happiness filling inside her. Patrick! Why hadn't she ever thought of him or really noticed him before? He was handsome and smart, popular, and probably the kindest boy in the entire junior class. And, she realized now, he'd had a crush on her for a long time.

Suddenly Meg heard her own breathing. It had grown very quiet in the front seat. She looked up and saw Nick staring back at her, his face strained and pale. When he caught her eye, he turned around again very fast and started the car.

"Nick," Darcy whined, "why are we leaving so soon?"

112

Nick didn't say a word as he pulled back onto the road, and Meg nestled against Patrick.

Sean floated into the bowling alley. He and Brooke walked in step, their hands clasped. The thud of the bowling balls and the crash of the pins sounded soft and easy, as if it were coming to him through warm water. Mostly he heard the Muzak rendition of an old Beatles song and some little kids laughing.

"They must be upstairs in the coffee shop," he told Brooke as he looked over the lanes.

"Let's go find them." She smiled.

"Okay."

They trotted up a spiral staircase carpeted in turquoise and pink. Again, they were in stride, like two well-trained ponies. At the top of the stairs was the smell of coffee and lots of echoey chatter.

"SEAN!! HEY, PENDLETON!!"

Sam Pond shot up and waved, his fuzzy head reflecting the fluorescent light. He was crammed in a booth with Jim Burke, from the yearbook staff; Kirstin Boldt, and two other gymnasts; and Joanne Fantozzi, a varsity cheerleader.

"Hey, Sam," Sean called back, making his way over with Brooke.

"You're just in time for the rematch," Sam told him. "Nick left, so you'll have to take over the Wombats."

"Me? Sure." Sean stood a little taller and smiled back at Brooke. "Where's Meg?"

"I think she left, too. A while ago. With Patrick Delancie."

"So who's going to be captain of the Aard-varks?"

"I am," announced a loud, firm voice from the booth behind them.

Sean turned around.

It was Celia. She was leaning on her elbows, surrounded by Maria Martinez, head of the debate club; Michael Chapman, a top tennis player; Phil Davidson, student body treasurer; and about six others. They were all huddled over as if Celia'd been telling them something secret and important. Everyone stared at Sean and Brooke. Celia's eyes looked hard and spiky, like blue-green coral. "Hi."

Brooke squeezed in front of Sean. "Hi, everybody. I'm Brooke Applebaum."

Sean suddenly realized that he hadn't intro-duced her at all. Brooke probably knew some of the people from classes, but not everybody. He went around Celia's table announcing each per-son's name. Brooke smiled and whispered hi, but they all answered her with cool nods. Instead of looking up, they stirred coffee or shredded napkins. Tension started to creep up Sean's back.

Brooke bravely parked herself in front of the booth and locked eyes with Celia. "You're Allie Simon's good friend, aren't you?"

Celia exchanged glances with other kids at the table.

"Is she okay?" Brooke went on. "I haven't seen her since she ran out of that audition. I called, but her mother said she didn't want to talk to anyone."

"What audition?" Celia demanded, sitting up.

"At school. For *Our Town*. I wanted to make sure Allie checked the call-back list. Her name is on it."

"Why wouldn't she check?"

"Well, she got upset and ran out. I couldn't go after her because I had to help Ms. Smith."

"So that's why Allie was even worse yesterday," Celia reasoned, looking at Maria. "And that's where she was going when we saw her after school on Thursday, and she acted so weird." Maria nodded angrily. Celia glared at Brooke. "I suppose that was your idea, having her go to that audition?"

"Well. . . ."

"Just like it was your idea to get her in trouble when we went to see that play."

Now everybody at the table was sitting up, accusing Brooke with their eyes.

"Now, wait a minute . . ." Sean objected.

Celia stood up and threw down her napkin. "Brooke, Allie is having a lot of problems. She needs to be around the right kind of people, and the last person she needs now is you." The others stood to let Celia out first. "Come on, everybody, let's go bowl." She looked right at Brooke. "Teams are already picked. If we add anybody else, it'll be uneven." Celia led the way downstairs and the others quickly followed.

Sean turned toward Brooke. The color was gone from her face, as if she'd been bleached under her freckles. But before he could say, "Celia's sure being a jerk," or "just stick with me," someone whacked his back with an open palm. The adrenaline shot into Sean's limbs, and his old instinct took over. Sean whipped around, ready to protect himself.

"So, Dr. Science," Sam was teasing, "you going to lead us to victory or not?" Sam took Sean's arm and pulled him toward the stairs. But Sean was still holding onto Brooke with his other hand, and she stood firm. He felt as if he was in the middle of a game of tug-of-war.

"Hold on a sec," Sean ordered Sam. He turned back to Brooke. "Brooke, will you come down and watch?" Sean tried to laugh. "We're pretty funny."

Brooke let go of Sean's hand as voices bubbled up from halfway down the stairs.

"Sean! We're waiting."

"Come on, fearless leader!"

"Hey, Dr. Science, how about some scientific invention so we win every time!"

"Grease for their shoes."

"Pins that won't fall down."

"How about just getting going so we can grab a decent lane."

"Really. Let's get a move on, Dr. Science."

"SEAAANNNN, LET'S GO!!!"

Sean looked back and forth between Brooke and the staircase. "Just one game. Afterward we can come back up here and get something to eat. Okay?"

Brooke didn't say anything. She just stood there, watching him.

Sam gave one more tug and Sean started down the stairs, the gravity pulling him faster and faster and farther away from Brooke. As soon as he hit

116

the bottom he was surrounded by his teammates who swept him along, arranging for a lane, renting shoes, setting up the score card, and flipping a coin to see who bowled first. By the time the game started, Sean was wearing Joanne's Wombat T-shirt and bantering with Sam. He kept looking around, hoping that Brooke would join them, but she didn't show. He wanted to go and find her, but he was captain so he couldn't leave, and besides, he knew it would get weird again if Brooke and Celia were together. He decided. He'd bowl with the gang, let them think everything was cool, and then go back to Brooke.

By the end of the game the Wombats were three points behind, and it was Sean's turn. "Here we go," he said, huffing on the bowling ball and shining it with his elbow, "the final chance for the Americans to defeat those Russian women with hairy armpits."

"Sean!!" giggled Celia and Maria at the same time.

Sean did a little dance, trying to prove that the scene upstairs hadn't bothered him. He let the ball go. It dribbled, it swerved, it almost went in the gutter and at the last moment, it knocked down five pins.

"WOMBATS WIN IT. ALL RIGHT!!!" screamed his team. They jumped all over him as if he'd just won the World Series.

"Two games out of three," insisted Celia and the rest of the Aardvarks. "Two out of three."

"You're such a sore loser." Sean gave a forced laugh.

Everybody laughed with him, then scattered to

117

get sodas, trade bowling balls, and set up for the next game.

Sean used his Wombat T-shirt to wipe the sweat from his forehead and rushed up to the main corridor to look for Brooke.

He saw her as soon as he got past the railing. She was sitting alone, cross-legged on the floor in front of a wall of red lockers, reading an old, beat-up copy of *Sports Illustrated*.

"Hi," he said crouching down next to her.

Brooke closed the magazine and put it aside.

Sean picked it up. It was about six months old and had a football player on the cover. "I didn't know you liked football."

"I don't," she said curtly. "I just found it. Is your game over?"

"Yeah. We won."

"Good." There was an angry sarcasm in her voice that hit Sean like a slap in the face.

"I'm sorry for kind of deserting you," he offered. "But I knew it was better than being around Celia. When she acts like that there's no getting through to her."

"Oh. Really." Brooke stood up and waited for Sam Pond and Jim Burke to walk by before speaking again. "I see." She wouldn't look at Sean. "Could you take me home?"

"Now?" Sean's stomach plunged.

She nodded and marched stiffly toward the exit.

Sean hurried to catch up with her. In the doorway he ran into Maria and Phil, who were coming back from outside.

They stared at Brooke as she shoved past them,

then turned on Sean. "Are you leaving?" Maria asked.

Sean could see Brooke through the glass. She was waiting next to his van, arms crossed, staring at the ground. He felt as if he was being ripped in half. "Uh. Yes. I'm not sure."

"Come on," Maria teased, "we have one more game." She giggled. "And we're going to make the Wombats beg for mercy this time." She clung to his arm.

Sean wriggled loose. "Go ahead without me. Tell Sam to take my place."

"Sean!" Maria objected, hands on her hips.

But Sean barely heard her as he rushed past and out into the parking lot. It was cold and crisp.

"Brooke, are you sure you want to go home?"

Brooke's hand was already on the door handle. "Very."

Sean unlocked the doors and they both climbed in. He started the van and drove in silence. They were halfway to Brooke's house before he looked at her. She was staring out her window, her usually animated face still and sad. A single tear crept down her cheek.

Sean pulled over and turned off the engine. He was suddenly so full of pain and frustration that he didn't think he could drive. He slid over and put his arm around her. She flinched and pushed him away.

"Brooke, I'm sorry. My friends just don't know you yet. And this whole thing with Allie is a misunderstanding. Give them some time."

She faced him. "Is that why you think I'm upset?"

"Isn't it?"

"No."

"Then, what is it?"

"I don't care about them."

"You don't?"

"They're not important. It's you. You're just not who I thought you were."

Sean's insides went hollow. "What do you mean?"

"I thought you were proud of being different, but you're not. All you want is to be just like them. If they don't like me, then you don't like me."

Sean felt as if his heart was being ripped out of him. "That's not true! I'm crazy about you! I've never felt this way about a girl before, ever."

She said in a firm voice, "You can't be crazy about me when we're alone, and embarrassed to be seen with me with your friends. It doesn't work that way."

Sean was so confused he didn't know what to say. But it didn't matter. She was in no mood to listen.

"Please take me home."

He drove on, barely seeing or hearing anything except the tears starting in his eyes and the pounding inside his head. Somehow he made it to her house. When he pulled up, he saw a big station wagon in the driveway. Three little girl faces popped into the kitchen window. And the sheep dog. Brooke got out before he could say anything.

"Brooke?" he called.

She stopped.

"Can I come over tomorrow so we can talk about it?"

She shook her head no.

"Can I call you?"

No, again.

"Brooke, I'm sorry."

She walked away. She didn't turn around or say good-night or even wave good-bye.

CHAPTER 11

Meg yawned. She rubbed her eyes. She spread her papers out over the library table and went over it again. The lobes of the brain. The skeleton. The muscles. She felt as if there was so much information crammed in her head it might leak out her ears.

The library was overheated, and she could vaguely smell the cafeteria kitchen down the hall. Even though school didn't start for another half hour, the tables were crowded. Friday mornings were like that. Everyone cramming, furiously scribbling on papers due that afternoon. Meg realized that her eyes were starting to close again and wished she hadn't left so much studying till the last minute.

The reason she'd had to cram was partly because of final planning for College Day. And partly because she'd lost her study partners. All week Nick had had extra track workouts, and

Sean had been so moody he'd barely talked to her. This was a really important and difficult exam, and she was beginning to wish she hadn't needed to pull an all-nighter.

Meg tried to keep her eyes open as she silently listed the parts of the ear. Someone slid into the chair next to her. She moved over to give him more room and tried not to break her concentration. But she was overwhelmed by the smell of tea, butter, and spinach.

It was Patrick.

"Hi," he whispered, hovering over her. He wore a navy parka that was so puffy it looked as if something was stuffed inside it.

"Hi."

He gave her an adoring smile. "Shhh! Don't let anybody catch us." He reached in his parka and took out a white paper sack. "I thought you might need this."

Meg opened it. "Oh, Patrick, thanks." Inside was a croissant filled with spinach and cheese, and a cup of strong, hot tea.

"I was going to get you some doughnuts, but I thought you might need protein — you know, brain food."

Meg took a secretive bite. Butter dripped down her hand. "Mmm. It's great."

"Did you stay up all night?"

She gulped down some tea. "All night."

Patrick leaned back, and Meg saw that his parka was still puffed out, and moving. "What else is in there?"

He grinned and unzipped to the middle of his chest. A scroungy gray terrior popped its head out. It started to bark but Patrick held its snout and shushed it. "He was in the street near the park. Two cars almost hit him. He doesn't have any tags." Patrick looked around. "I'd better take him home. I can figure out what to do with him later." He gently pushed the dog back against his chest and pulled up the zipper. "When's your test?"

"Third period."

"You'll do great. I'll find you at lunch. I think everything's under control for College Day. Will you be there right after school?"

"As soon as I can."

He backed up, but hesitated before leaving. "Did you decide if you wanted to do something tonight, after College Day?" He looked down shyly, patting the top of the puppy's head.

Meg stalled. "I'd better just go home and sleep. If I stay awake through the rest of today, it'll be a miracle."

Patrick tried not to look disappointed. "Maybe we'll do something really special next weekend, then."

"Yeah."

He stared at her for a few more seconds, as if he couldn't tear himself away. "I'll think of something. I guess I'd better let you study." The puppy yapped again and Patrick hurried out.

Meg tried to go back to her books, but all she could see in those diagrams was Patrick's sweet, open face. Since Saturday night he'd called her twice a day, stuck notes and poems in her locker, brought her a rose at the College Day planning meeting, and waited for her between almost every class.

She wasn't sure what to do. She liked him. She respected him. She was even attracted to him. She just didn't know if she liked him as much as he liked her. It was a little scary, this flood of attention. She'd had no idea what she was getting into when she'd impulsively kissed him in the back of Nick's car.

This whole week she'd avoided thinking seriously about Patrick. She'd told herself that she had too many other things on her mind. Soon midterms and College Day would be over, and then she would figure out what was really going on between her and Patrick. Suddenly glad for the distraction of bones and nerve endings, Meg pulled her books in closer and continued to study.

"Allie, you didn't tell us that we were invited to College Day!"

"You didn't even tell us there was a College Day!"

The Volvo flowed smoothly through traffic. The engine was superquiet and so was Allie. She figured that her father and mother were huffing and sighing enough for all of them. Allie wished for a sudden sputter from the radiator or an explosion from the tires. If only the car had a mind of its own and would decide to turn around and go back to the garage. If only the Volvo would go anywhere other than where it was going — school and this stupid, pointless thing called College Day.

"Your mother wouldn't even have known about it," Mr. Simon lectured, "if she hadn't found that invitation in the trash."

"Allie," her mom said in a softer voice, "why did you throw it away without showing it to me?"

Allie curled up in the back so tightly that her seat belt pinched. She didn't look at her mother but gazed out the window instead.

"Allie, are you listening?"

"I'm listening!"

They coasted to a stoplight. Mrs. Simon turned around. She was wearing a blue business suit with a pink scarf that reminded Allie of her little sister's baby clothes. Allie knew what was coming — the pretend-to-be-nice-and-understanding tactic.

Sure enough, her mother was right there. "Sweetheart, if I'd known, I could have gotten off at the bank early," she said in a soothing voice. "Your father is just meeting with students this afternoon, he doesn't have any classes. We would have wanted to come."

"Gee, thanks," Allie threw back sarcastically.

Her father threw up one of his hands, and it hit the visor so that his sunglasses fell into his lap. He angrily flipped them up onto the dashboard. "I can't believe you would deliberately hide that invitation from us like that. I've about had enough of this, Allie." The being nice tactic hadn't worked. Now he was trying tactic two: getting tough. "This is an opportunity for you to get information about the future. Aren't you even interested?"

Allie put her hands over her ears. She hated

hearing about opportunities and the future. She was tired of being told what an underachiever she was: how she should start living up to her potential. Didn't they understand that the only potential she had anymore was the one for screwing up?

"Not particularly," she argued. "Maybe I don't even want to go to college."

Her father swerved out of traffic, pulling over about half a block before the campus. She could see the top of his bald head turning red from anger, which didn't surprise her. Not going to college was, to him, like being a drug addict or getting sent to the state pen. Worse.

Before he could say anything, Allie decided to provoke him further. "Maybe I won't even finish high school. Maybe I'll just get my GED."

Now her mother whipped around, too, and they were both crimson.

"Don't even think about it," her father growled.

Her mother gave him a quick glance and took over. Back to tactic one. "Allie, we love you. We know you are going through a rough time. But you have to give things a chance. You shouldn't be on the defensive all the time."

"I'm not on the defensive. I do give things a chance. You're the ones not giving me the chance."

"Look, young lady," her father threatened, his voice starting to rise, "you're going to go to College Day this afternoon and walk around like a human being and get information about at least three schools. Before you know it, you'll be graduating and out in the world, on your own. . . ."

Allie ignored the shock the word "graduating" sent through her and argued, "Good! That's just what I want! I want to be out in the world, away from everybody who tells me what I have to do and how I have to act and dress. I want to be on my own. Not in some stupid high school cafeteria, talking about my stupid future!"

"That does it!" her father yelled back, slamming his fist on the top of the seat. "You will go to College Day this afternoon if I have to personally escort you there. Is that what you want?"

"Dad, no."

"I've had it up to here with you lately. Either you go by yourself and open your eyes to what's waiting for you in the world, or I will meet you at your last period class and drag you over there kicking and screaming."

"You would do something like that, wouldn't you?"

"To show you something about the way the world really operates, you bet I would, Allie. I'd do anything!"

"I know the way the world operates! When are you going to see that I'm not a baby! All I want is for everybody to leave me alone!"

"I'll leave you alone, all right, I'll — "

"STOP IT, YOU TWO!" her mother suddenly screamed.

Allie and her father were both quiet.

Mrs. Simon grabbed a tissue from the box on the dash and pressed it to her face.

Allie was filled with shame. Her mother's tears made her feel sick inside — mean and worthless.

128

She reached for the door handle but her father had the child-proof lock on.

"Dad, will you let me out?"

"Are you going this afternoon?" he insisted.

"Yes," Allie mumbled. "Would you open the door?"

"What did you say? I didn't hear you."

"Yes. YES. YES, I'M GOING!!"

The lock let loose and Allie flew out. She stumbled, then ran toward campus, her boots digging into the grass, something sharp in her bag stabbing her back. She looked back once to see the Volvo slowly pull back into traffic and glide away.

When she arrived at the parking lot she was stunned at how carefree and cheerful everyone else looked, as if high school were one big party. The flag fluttered in the wind, a car stereo blared, kids laughed and flirted and yelled to each other across the asphalt. Across the entrance was a huge sign advertising College Day.

Allie took a few steps toward the gate. Then she saw a bunch of girls gathered around Maria Martinez's station wagon. They were all giggling and whispering. Right in the middle was Celia all in white and pale yellow like those baby chicks they sold at Easter time.

Allie backed away before they could spot her, before they could wave her over and pretend they wanted her to join them. She'd seen it, how as each day went by, even Celia was getting less interested in saving her. Celia didn't really want Allie around any more than L.P. did or Mrs. Weaver or her parents.

Allie felt her jacket pocket for a cigarette. She didn't find one but instead felt the edges of something crisp and hopeful. A twenty-dollar bill. She'd stuck it in there after she'd blown that audition last week in case it came to this, in case she couldn't face it one more day.

What was she waiting for? She could go to school and see Celia and Meg, and even go to College Day to keep her parents happy. Or she could take her twenty dollars to the bus station and go somewhere where she could finally be on her own.

Allie didn't have to think twice. She stuffed the bill back in her pocket, left Redwood High, and headed downtown.

CHAPTER 12

"That's the femur."

"And you, Meg, have great femurs."

"Right, Nick. How about your knee."

"Um, the patella."

"Shin."

"Tibia? Or is it fibula. Shoot."

"One's in the front, one's in the back . . . I think."

"Yeah, but which is which?"

"You would have to ask that."

Meg and Nick had run into each other on the way to third period. Their physiology test would start in less than five minutes. Crammed to the gills with the names of bones and muscles, they were both tired, nervous, and slightly spacy. Nick almost leaned into her as they walked, while Meg relentlessly went over the last-minute scratch she'd made for the test. She was relieved that both of them were preoccupied with this exam.

She hadn't seen much of him since Saturday night and was hoping never to have to discuss that weird car ride.

Nick yawned as they ducked under a poster advertising the next swim meet and dodged kids rushing in both directions.

"You tired?"

Nick nodded. "I studied until four, and then it seemed like I'd just have to wake up in two more hours, so I never went to sleep."

"Me, either."

"So is it the tibia in the front and the fibula in the back?"

"I think so." They stopped across the hall from the physiology classroom. "Here comes Sean. Let's ask him."

Meg and Nick flattened themselves against the lockers and waved Sean over. He walked slowly, dragging his feet. His bowling shirt was untucked and his expression listless.

"Hey, how's your gluteus maximus?" Nick teased, giving Sean a kick in the rear.

"Cute," Sean responded flatly.

"Lighten up. You ready for this killer?"

Sean shrugged.

"He'll probably get the highest grade and ruin the curve for the rest of us," Meg teased.

Sean did not smile.

"Are you going to College Day after school?" Nick asked.

"Of course," Sean answered.

Nick and Meg looked at one another, reacting to Sean's grumpiness. But before they could ask

Sean for help with the tibia/fibula debate, there was a shout from the other end of the hallway. Celia was waving and trying to fight her way upstream through a bunch of burly guys who were on the wrestling team. As soon as she approached, Sean put down his head and hustled into the physiology room.

"Hi," Celia panted, not noticing that Sean had run off to avoid seeing her.

"Hi."

"So what's up?"

Celia dropped her smile. "Have you seen Allie?"

"Cici," Nick sighed, "believe it or not I have other things on my mind right now besides Allie."

"I know," Celia snapped. "It's just that she wasn't in English first period."

"Maybe she's sick."

Celia shook her head. "I called her last night."

"How'd she sound?"

"Terrible. I mean, actually she wouldn't even talk to me. I just talked to her mom. But she wasn't sick."

Meg folded her arms around her notebook. "Maybe she went to the dentist."

"Or maybe her mom let her stay home and watch game shows," Nick interrupted. "She hasn't been looking too happy to be back at old Redwood High." He started to leave. "Look, we have to go. If I think about anything else right now, I may forget every single thing I've been stuffing in my brain for the last twenty-four hours."

Celia fretted.

"I'm sure there's no reason to worry," Meg said, stifling a yawn. "Allie probably just woke up with a sore throat or something."

"You really think she's okay?" Celia asked.

Nick moved a little closer to Meg so he could scan her scratch sheet. "She's fine. But if Meg and I don't get going, we may be in big trouble."

The bell rang, and Meg quickly walked over to the trash can and let the scratch sheet float down out of her hand. Nick made a horrible face as if he had just been stabbed in the heart, then turned back to Celia. "Worry about us, not Allie," he told her. "We're the ones about to be tortured."

"Let's go, Rhodes," Meg teased. "Get your metatarsals moving. We've got to go take that test."

"You're sure I shouldn't worry?" Celia called over the crowd.

"WE'RE SURE," Meg and Nick yelled back at the same time.

Celia waved and the three friends split.

The air went out of the bus brakes with a giant whoosh, and the door swung open. After a two-hour ride, Allie stepped into the bus station in downtown San Francisco. No more smelly bus with lumpy seats and old ladies crumpling candy wrappers. No more freeways and bridges and feeling cramped and creepy about who was going to sit next to her. No more motion sickness and wondering if this bus was ever really going to get her where she wanted to go.

Allie made her way through the station, which smelled like old smoke and dirty bathrooms.

There were people everywhere — at the ticket lines, the food counters, on the floor and benches. A few were surrounded by bundles, and Allie saw one guy picking through a bin of trash. He caught her staring at him and rolled up his stocking cap to glare back. Allie walked faster.

As soon as she found her way out to the street she was engulfed by sweet ocean air, the chatter of different languages, the roar of cars, and the far-off echo of a trolley bell. Allie almost cried, she was so overwhelmed with hope and freedom. This wasn't like New York, with her parents hovering and her classmates scoffing at her. And it wasn't Redwood Hills, with her old friends pressuring her and the rest whispering and staring. This was Allie on her own. Making her way. Alone.

She stood on the corner and tried to get her bearings. There was an old hotel, fast-food places, a flower stall, clothing stores, a shop that sold dance costumes with sequins and feathers, and a huge parking garage. Beyond was more lively traffic, rows and rows of sand-colored buildings, and long, endless hills.

Allie knew where she wanted to go — the theater they'd visited on their field trip. It was right downtown, not far from the bus station. But which direction? She didn't recognize anything right around her and she didn't want to ask anyone, so she stuffed her hands in the pockets of her NO FUTURE jacket, pulled it more tightly around herself, and began to walk.

At first she followed the cable car tracks, along Union Square Park, past the fancy department stores and hotels. She walked up and down hills so steep they made her calves ache. Then she realized she was heading into a rundown neighborhood and away from downtown. She switched direction, putting her head down to avoid being noticed as she passed noisy bars and corner groceries, crumbly-looking apartment buildings, and laundromats. She was climbing uphill again when she saw a sign for Geary Street. After rounding the corner, there it was, the theater banner snapping in the wind. She happily jogged toward it, laughing to herself as she realized that she'd walked a huge square only to come back to within blocks of where she started.

She had been thinking a lot about the old man who'd let her and Brooke in to look around backstage. She was betting he would let her in again. Glancing quickly to see if anybody noticed her, Allie slipped down the passageway that led to the back of the old theater. There was an overflowing Dumpster and two cats and some graffiti sprayed on the walls. Finally she stood face to face with the stage door. She'd made it.

She knocked. There was no answer right away so she waited, listening carefully for footsteps inside. She knocked again. Harder this time. Still no answer. She pounded so hard she made her knuckles hurt. Nothing. No one. She folded onto the cold steel steps for a while and hugged her knees.

Not sure what else to do, she finally went back around, entering the narrow lobby from the street. The ticket windows were open, but there was no performance that afternoon and, besides, she didn't have enough money to buy a ticket. So she stared at the actors' pictures posted on the lobby walls, memorizing each name, each face. Finally she took a program from a stack near the wall — the same program she'd kicked at Mrs. Weaver — slumped down on the worn carpet and read it, cover to cover . . . five times.

"You can't sit here all day, you know."

Allie first saw the shined shoes, then the wool slacks, sweater, and bow tie. It was the man from behind the ticket window.

"What?" Allie scrambled to her feet.

"Are you waiting for someone?"

"No."

"Then you can't sit here all day. Shouldn't you be in school?"

At the word "school," Allie grabbed her bag and ran back into the street. It was cooler now and not so bright. The exhaust was thick, and a car horn seemed to blare every five seconds. A city bus was heading into the empty lane where she stood, and she bolted across the street, swerving to avoid a taxi and a motorcycle. She stopped in front of a posh delicatessen. Now what? There were still two hours before her bus back and she only had six dollars to spare, saving the seven she needed for the ride home.

She walked and walked, but the hills were so steep, and her legs were getting tired. Her hands stung from the cold, and she was afraid of getting too far from the bus station and not being able to find her way back. More and more people seemed to be rushing along the sidewalk, so that if she slowed down they bumped into her or pushed her aside. And they looked at her as if she were nothing . . . a fly, a smudge, a little irritation to be swatted aside.

Finally Allie stepped into the entranceway of an old apartment house, five square feet of dirty tile and mailboxes. She was only a few blocks from Geary Street, back in the neighborhood of the loud bars and crummy laundromats. All she wanted was to stand in one place for a moment and rest. She cocked one foot against the wall, hugged her bag to her chest, and wondered if anyone else in the world had ever been so totally and completely alone.

Suddenly the front door of the apartment swung open and a young man appeared, not much older than she. Half his head was shaved, the other half sprouted an orangy-red ponytail. He wore a leather jacket, baggy jeans, and no shirt. As soon as he saw her, he whipped around and slapped his palms against the wall, pinning her between his bare chest and the row of mailboxes. Allie froze with panic. All she could smell was sweaty leather and her own fear.

His eyes were bloodshot and his skin pasty. He looked at her as if he recognized her, as if her clothes and dyed hair made her a sister or an old friend.

"Hey, what's going on?" he said, his face in hers.

"Leave me alone."

He laughed. "What's the matter? You going to Jack's?"

"What?"

"JACK'S!" he yelled in her ear, and then

laughed again, amused by his own joke. "Yeah, Jack's. There's lots of folks up there. I bet he'd let you stay if you want."

Allie started to cry.

"He always lets the girls stay."

"Please leave me alone," she pleaded.

He stared at her, his eyes focusing, confused by her tears.

She pushed against his arm but he wouldn't let her go. "If you don't let me go, I'll scream."

He laughed again.

"I'll call the police!"

"Go ahead."

"I will," she sobbed, beating against his forearm with her fist. He caught her wrist, but she twisted it away and ducked under his other arm, breaking free. She ran.

As she tore down the street she heard him call after her, "I DON'T CARE!!!!"

Allie scrambled down the crowded sidewalk like Nick making a brilliant play in a football game. Tears streamed down her face, but she barely felt them. She was too scared, and her heart was throbbing too hard for her to be aware of anything else.

She reached Geary Street and headed back toward the theater. Before she reached it, she passed a coffee shop with a long front counter and round booths, like a big Denny's. She flung open the glass door and stood in the entrance gasping for breath.

A middle-aged woman with a huge, sprayed hairdo came over. She looked Allie up and down.

"Can I sit in here?" Allie managed.

"You gonna eat?"

Eat. Food. Allie suddenly realized that she was starving. Famished. Totally empty. "Yes. Please."

The woman led her to a table by the window, swung on a tablecloth, and slapped down a menu.

Allie didn't open it. She checked the clock on the wall. She had forty minutes before her bus home. There wasn't another one to Redwood Hills until tomorrow. She didn't want to miss that bus for anything in the world. She stopped the waitress before the woman could go back to the counter. "I'm sort of in a hurry. Can I just order now?"

The woman shrugged. "Sure."

Allie ordered a hamburger and a Coke. Then she stared out the window and waited for the boy to come after her.

He didn't. Her food came and with each bite she checked the street again. He was gone. Allie began to feel safer as she filled up with food and the time for her bus grew closer.

The waitress came by once more to press the check onto the table cloth. Allie picked it up as she rose. But after she looked at it she fell back into her seat and her terror returned.

Nine dollars! How could anyone charge nine dollars for a hamburger and a Coca-Cola? If she paid nine dollars, she wouldn't have enough money to buy her bus ticket home! Allie grabbed a menu from the next table, sure there was some kind of mistake. But it was true. Everything on the menu cost over twice what Allie would have expected.

Allie stared at the check and at the thirteen

dollars left in her purse. Thirteen. How perfect. Her life had become one big number thirteen. She rested her face on the tablecloth and thought about the fact that she was at the end. Her luck had totally run out.

CHAPTER 13

College Day was a huge success. The cafeteria echoed with the scraping of chairs against linoleum, two hundred voices talking and calling, brochures being passed out, and pencils scribbling down information. Over half the junior class had turned out, plus some seniors, teachers, and parents, and of course the representatives from each college were behind their tables.

Some of the lines were so long that Celia and Meg had joined forces, splitting up to hit more tables and pool their information. Besides, Meg was so punchy by now that Celia figured if she didn't point her in the right direction, Meg might curl up in a corner and go to sleep. Returning from their latest mission, they wiggled their way back into the center of the room, both holding messy handfuls of paper over their heads.

"Here, Cici," Meg called over the noise. "My dad got these for you at the San Francisco State table." She handed Celia a fat pamphlet and some printed sheets. "There's info there on studying business, marketing, and interior design. Oh, and I picked up some sheets for you about a fashion school in LA. I didn't know if you'd be interested in it or not."

"Thanks." Celia stuffed the brochures in her notebook and handed some to Meg. "This is pre-med stuff from Berkeley. Did your parents leave?"

Meg nodded as she opened the Berkeley pamphlet. "They had to get back to work. I saw Sean's dad at the very beginning, but he left, too. Sean is still over at the Cal Tech table."

Celia turned Meg around so she could lean her notebook on Meg's back and make some notes. "I hope Sean's nicer to the people from Cal Tech than he's been to everybody else lately."

"Do you know what he's so uptight about?"

Celia shrugged and kept writing. Of course, she suspected that Sean's moodiness had to do with Brooke Applebaum. She hadn't seen them together since the bowling alley, and she knew that Sean partly blamed her. But eventually he would thank her.

"Allie never showed up, did she?"

Celia's insides got even tighter at the mention of Allie. She figured that Meg and Nick were right — Allie was probably just home with a runny nose. Celia'd almost called at lunchtime, but she didn't want Allie to think she was bugging her. As with Sean, it was becoming more and more obvious that Allie didn't appreciate her concern. Still, Celia told herself, she was being a good friend — to both Allie and Sean. She was looking out for both of their best interests.

Meg suddenly put a hand over her mouth, stifling laughter. "Look at that." She pointed "That's the Bradley table."

The Bradley College table was set up near the window, and amidst the crowd and commotion, it stood empty. Their brochures were still neatly stacked and the representative stared up at the ceiling, as if he were counting the holes in the acoustical tile.

"Uh-oh," Meg giggled. "Is Darcy here?"

"Of course. I saw her a little while ago, dragging Nick around. He looks like he's ready to fall asleep, too." Celia finished writing, and Meg turned around.

"Cici, look. The Redwood College line is still about a mile long. Who gets to tackle that one?"

Celia was about to volunteer when she looked over at the Bradley table again and saw a shadowy figure standing in the hall, rapping on the window and waving. At first she thought it was one of her classmates or an underclassman trying to impress her friends by being on friendly terms with the juniors. Then she looked again and saw the bright orange dress, the layered and frosted hair, the searching eyes ringed with dark pencil. Her stomach fell. Her mother! Her mother was standing in the hall, for the Class of '88 to gawk and giggle at.

Celia tried to stay calm. She didn't want to draw any more attention than necessary. "Meg, would you mind taking the Redwood line? I have to go outside for a second."

144

Meg looked a little puzzled, but shrugged sleepily. "Okay."

"I'll be right back."

"Sure."

Celia hurried out. Hopefully, most kids would think her mother was a senior or a student teacher with trashy taste. Whatever made her show up here, after all the fights they'd had about it! At least there wasn't anybody else in the hall.

Mrs. Cavenaugh was leaning against the door to the faculty lounge, examining her painted nails. When she saw Celia coming toward her, she stood with her hip slung to one side and her arms crossed, as prepared for an argument as Celia was.

"Mom," Celia stressed in a muffled, angry voice. "I asked you not to come. Why are you doing this to me?"

Her mother held up a hand to stop her. "Celia, cool down. I'm not trying to humiliate you by my horrible presence, okay?"

"You promised you wouldn't come. I don't believe you'd do this." Celia knew the yelling could start any second. Desperate to avoid a scene, she pulled her mother into a niche in the hall where the janitors stowed their mops and buckets.

"Celia, I'm not crazy about being here and having you treat me like this, either."

"Then why did you come?"

Her mom hesitated, then looked Celia straight in the face. Her eyes were dead serious behind the dark mascara. "It's Allie."

"Allie?"

"She called."

"What?"

"Something's wrong."

Celia interrupted with a gasp. "I knew it. I knew there was a bad reason she wasn't in school. What did she say? When did she call? Where is she?"

"Celia, if you give me a chance, I'll tell you."

"Okay, okay."

"She called about fifteen minutes ago. She sounded like she might have been crying."

"What did she say?"

"Not much. She wanted to talk to you. Then she said something about being alone, about being sick of being alone. When I asked her, she said she was all right, but she wanted you to come and meet her, or pick her up, I couldn't tell which. Then she hung up."

"Pick her up where?"

"I have no idea."

"Mom! Didn't you ask her?"

"Celia, she was on for less than a minute. The TV was on. She wasn't making much sense. I could barely hear her."

"Did you call her parents?"

Her mother shrugged and scraped the floor with her high heel. "No. I'm sure they're both still at work. Besides, Allie begged me not to. You know how they are, they'll call out the National Guard or something. Allie might just be wandering around town somewhere. I thought we could look for her first. If we don't find her by five, then we definitely tell her folks."

"You mean, you'll help?" Celia asked in a very soft voice.

Her mother wouldn't quite look at her. "Of course."

For a moment Celia couldn't speak. "What should we do?"

"I thought you and I would check downtown and the mall. Have Nick and Sean and Meg look any other places they think she might be."

"Okay."

"Go tell your friends. I'll wait for you in the parking lot." Mrs. Cavenaugh started down the hall, her high heels clattering.

Celia watched her. From the back she looked about seventeen years old. Just before her mom reached the door, Celia called out, "Mom!"

Her mother stopped and turned back, ready for another fight.

"Mom, I uh, I just wanted to say . . . thanks."

Mrs. Cavenaugh stared at Celia, then sadly shook her head. "Get Nick, Meg, and Sean. Hurry." She waved and rushed out.

As quickly as she could, Celia cut her way back through the crowd. She pulled Meg out of the Redwood College line, dragged Nick away from Darcy, and found Sean still talking to the representative from Cal Tech. They were all confused and annoyed at being interrupted until they found out that Allie was in trouble. As soon as they heard that, they huddled around Celia in a corner and tried to figure out how to help.

They stood between the flag and a stack of extra chairs. "I have the van. I'll drive around the neighborhoods," Sean suggested right away. "Maybe she's just out walking."

Nick took Meg's arm. "Maybe you and I

should hike the woods behind my house."

"Okay," Meg nodded. "I have to get some stuff in my locker. It'll take me two seconds. I'll meet you at your car."

Nick looked from face to face to face. "Let's all meet at my house by dinnertime. If we still haven't found her, we'll have to tell her parents by then."

"Right."

Celia, Meg, and Sean started to make their way through the crowd. Nick stacked his college brochures against his side, and headed into the crowd. His head was suddenly filled with Allie — what happened to her? Was she all right? Why hadn't he realized earlier that something was wrong? He rudely wedged his way through long lines and in between conversations. He even crawled under one table to take a shortcut to the door. But before he made it out, a head of shiny chestnut hair popped up in front of him, blocking his way. Darcy.

She was wearing a jumpsuit and her riding boots and stood with her hands on her hips like some kind of military guard. "Nick, where are you going?"

"Home."

Her smile vanished. "You're leaving?"

"Yeah, Darce. I have to."

"What did the guy from Bradley say?"

"I didn't talk to him."

"What!"

"Darce, come on. I don't really care about Bradley. I've gotta go."

She rolled her eyes, then grabbed his arm, and

started to drag him over, as if he were a reluctant little boy. "You're not leaving without talking to Bradley College." She was trying to sound playful.

He whipped his hand away with such force that Darcy spun around angrily to face him, her face full of shock.

"Allie's in trouble," he explained. "I need to go help look for her."

"In trouble how?"

"I don't know. I have to go, Darce."

Darcy's face suddenly scrunched up with petulance and anger. "Who told you about this? Meg McCall? I bet it's just an excuse so Meg can get you alone. That's just about her style."

"What? What are you talking about?" Nick backed up, smashing into a college rep and a set of parents. He almost felt like laughing. Suddenly it all seemed so meaningless. Bradley College and dumb parties. Track and Darcy and all the other dumb girls he'd dated junior year.

Darcy followed him, twisting a hank of hair against her mouth, as if she was changing her approach. Sure enough, she pressed against him with her most seductive smile. She wound her arms around him and started kissing him slowly up the side of his neck. Nick held her shoulders and pried her away.

"Oh, come on, Nick! I know Allie is an old friend and all, but she's screwed up. And she's not your problem."

"Yes, she is."

"Why?"

"I don't know," Nick stammered, backing away.

Darcy stamped the floor with her riding boot and pointed a finger at him. "I'm telling you, Nick, if you leave this cafeteria without talking to that man from Bradley College, that's it for you and me. Understand"

"You mean it?" Nick tossed back, with a tiny smile.

"Yes!"

"See you 'round," he said, and with a wave, he bolted for the door.

He ran as fast as he could until he reached the parking lot, where he stood next to his car and waited for Meg. He wasn't sure why he felt so free all of a sudden. He wasn't sure why it was so important that he go after Allie. All he knew was that it had to do with something complicated and deep and not always fun or satisfying. Something his life had been lacking lately. Something called love.

CHAPTER
14

Brooke shoved aside the ant farm and the Rubik's cube, the chewed tennis ball and Daphne's Breathblaster from the top of her living room coffee table. She slapped down a stack of college brochures in their place and began sorting through them.

"Great, here's a school with a major in pulp and paper. That sounds perfect for me."

She plowed through some more, discarding a few as if they were Frisbees. "Waste management. Mortuary science. Oh, it's a great future out there for weirdos like me. Maybe I should just join the circus."

Rex, the sheep dog, lumbered over. He slobbered on her, then looked up sweetly, as if Brooke were talking to him. No one else was home. "That's another weird thing about me," she told the dog, "I talk to myself."

She stretched out on the sofa, kicking aside a

few pillows and her father's fishing vest. She'd been the first one at College Day and had run from table to table like a contestant on *Supermarket Sweep* — this old game show her mother talked about, where housewives had minutes to grab as many free groceries as they could. She'd been that eager to gather college information and get out of the cafeteria before she had to see Sean or any of his friends.

"Darn!" she yelped suddenly. Rex jumped up on her and she held him around the neck, groaning and burying her face in his fur. She'd decided. No matter how much it hurt, she and Sean were through. It had taken her too long to get confidence in herself, to trust that it was okay to be Brooke Applebaum. She wasn't going to throw it all away just because, for the first time in her sixteen years, she had fallen in love.

"Ohhhh," she cried. Why did this have to be so painful? Why couldn't she graduate tomorrow so she'd never have to see Sean or his friends ever again? Why did she have to feel as if she was going nuts every time she passed Sean in the hall? She hugged Rex harder and slammed her fist against the back of the couch. Why did it have to work out this way! Why had her parents raised her to be a freak! Her last groan was answered by the doorbell.

"No one's home!" she yelled. It was probably one of her sisters, who would yell back something stupid and then let herself in with the key under the flowerpot.

But the bell kept ding-donging until Brooke wanted to scream. By the time she got up, Rex was jumping and howling, and the phone had started to ring.

"Oh, great," she muttered. "Maybe the oven timer and the alarm clock will go off, too." She picked up the phone, put her hand over the mouthpiece and yelled as the doorbell rang again and again. "I'M COMING!" She went back to the phone. "Hang on," she said, before the caller could get a word in, "there's somebody at the door." She slammed the phone down on the kitchen table, just missing a crusty bowl of rice pudding, and ran around the front hall to the door.

When she turned the knob, the door pushed open as if there were five people leaning on the other side. Sean stumbled toward her, his face red, and his hair falling over his forehead. She jumped back as if he were made of hot coals.

"Go away!" she demanded.

"Brooke, I can't stand it. I have to talk to you."

"There's nothing to talk about."

"Brooke, please!" He raised his hands to his face as Rex started jumping up on him, licking and barking.

"That's right, Rex, get him!" she commanded. Rex immediately calmed down and padded away.

"I know you never want to see me again," Sean continued breathlessly, "but I've been driving around the streets, looking for Allie. And I can't find Allie, but I do keep finding your house. And I just thought maybe I could talk to you for a few minutes because I'm an incredible jerk and if I could only explain why I'm such a jerk maybe you'd — "

"That's right. You are a jerk."

His freckled face went slack and his arms went limp at his sides. "I know. Oh, Brooke, I'm sorry."

For a moment they both stood there, on either side of the doorway, staring down at their feet.

Brooke broke away. "I'm on the phone."

When she went back to the telephone, Sean stayed in the doorway as if he was a magazine salesman.

Brooke picked up the phone again, but she could barely concentrate enough to listen.

"Yes."

"Hello?" The voice was faint, partly covered by static and the honking of car horns.

"Who's this?"

"Brooke? Is this you? Please be home, Brooke."

Brooke pressed her ear closer to the phone. There was something about the thin, frightened voice, the strange pleading for her to be home, that pulled her attention away from Sean.

"Yes, this is Brooke."

"Oh, I'm so glad you're home. This is Allie. Allie Simon."

Sean had crept into the hallway, and Brooke suddenly remembered him saying something about looking for Allie. She looked up at Sean and covered the mouthpiece with her hand. "It's Allie," she whispered.

Sean rushed over. He tried to grab the phone, but Brooke wouldn't let him.

"Find out where she is!" he urged. "Tell her we'll go get her."

Brooke glared at him, then went back to the phone. "Allie, where are you?"

154

"I'm in San Francisco, at the corner of Geary and Powell, where the cable car stops, near the theater. I don't have enough money to get home. I can't face calling my parents. I know it's a lot to ask, and that we don't know each other that well, but I really want to come home. I'm all alone here. I know you care and I'm afraid. I'm afraid of not caring . . . oh, I can't explain it, but could you come and get me? Please!"

Sean was pressed up against Brooke, sharing the receiver. She turned her back to him and tried to ignore the closeness of his body to hers. He nodded and mimed for her to tell Allie yes.

"Of course I'll come get you," Brooke told Allie. She pulled the phone away from Sean. "Stay right there. I'm leaving now, so I'll be there around five-thirty."

"Oh, Brooke, thanks. I'll be in the Regal Coffee Shop. It's right on the corner."

"I'll be there as soon as I can."

Brooke hung up the phone and started scribbling a note for her parents. When she went to gather her sweater and book bag, she saw Sean pick up her phone again and punch the buttons. He waited, then slammed the phone down and tried another number.

"Who are you calling?"

Sean barely looked up. "Her folks. Celia. I guess I'll try Nick's." He punched some more. "Darn. Nobody's home. Well, let's go. We can stop and call again on the way."

"We?"

Sean was getting out his car keys and leading

the way to the door. "Yeah. We. It's okay. I'll drive."

Brooke plowed through the front door and faced him furiously on the steps. "Who says I want to be stuck in a car with you all the way to San Francisco!"

"It's a van."

"What?"

"A van. I have my parents' van."

"I don't care if it's a mobile home. Allie called me, and I'm going to get her. By myself."

Sean stood in front of her, blocking her access to the rusty old Rambler her grandfather had given her. It barely made it up Capitola Mountain, let alone up and down the hills of San Francisco. But Brooke tried not to think about that as she pushed Sean aside and tried to open the door.

"You can't go alone. It'll be dark soon. It's a long drive."

"So what?"

"So, you shouldn't drive all that way alone."

"Watch me!"

"No, thanks. Watching you in driver's ed was bad enough. If you drive like you used to drive that simulator, I'd better call out the highway patrol!"

Brooke found the corner of her mouth rising in a tiny smile. Sean grabbed her elbow and started pulling her into the street.

"Oh, all right." Brooke swung open the door to the van and climbed in. When Sean hesitated, standing on the curb, and gazing at her, she yelled, "Well, come on, Pendleton. What are you waiting for? Let's go!"

156

* * *

Meg and Nick had walked and walked. Past the old tree house, up and down the trails, through the woods, around the pond, back and forth across the long grass. They were all the way to the edge of the Barricelli Vineyard. The light was starting to slip away, and it was getting cold. There was no trace of Allie.

"Maybe we should just go back," Meg said. Strong as she was, she'd never been able to go without sleep. Her limbs felt like jelly, and her mind was clouded. She could barely keep her balance.

Nick had no such problem. He was suddenly wired, more full of life than she'd seen him all year. While she waited, he shimmied up the trunk of an old oak to look out over the vineyard and the woods. "Shoot. I don't see anybody." He swung on a branch, jumped down, and jogged back over to her. "I still have this feeling she might be out here, though. I saw her come walking back through our yard at least twice last week."

Meg cupped her hands around her mouth, leaned back her head, and called weakly, *"Aaallllllliieeeeeeee."*

The only response was a soft wind and the rustle of leaves. Meg stepped back to call again but stepped on a fallen branch. Her ankle twisted and she started to stumble.

Nick caught her. He clutched her waist and when she looked up, his face was inches from hers. His cheeks reddened, and he gently slid his hands to her shoulders to steady her. He smiled. For a moment the only thing she could see was the brilliant green of his eyes. He reached up and took a small stick out of her hair.

"Oh, Meg," he said in an intense voice.

Meg pulled away. She somehow found the energy to scramble ahead through the brush. Nick caught up and jogged beside her, still watching her with the strangest smile. Their feet crunched leaves and branches until they reached a small clearing, and Nick went off into some thick woods to call again. He hooted, hollered, and whistled. Hughie, back at the house, barked.

Meg folded onto the ground, leaning back against a tree stump. She couldn't figure out why Nick was flying so high when all she felt was weariness and worry. But she was too tired to think about it for long. Nick quickly returned and crouched down next to her.

"You okay?" he asked, squinting up at the darkening sky.

"Fine."

"How about if we just sit here for a few minutes. Maybe we keep missing her. If we sit in one place for a while, maybe she'll find us."

"Great." Meg settled back against the stump. Nick immediately inched closer and put his arm over her shoulder. At first Meg moved back, but she was too tired for much resistance or thought. Finally, she let her head fall onto his shoulder.

"You're really tired, aren't you."

"Yeah."

"Go ahead and close your eyes. Lean on me. I'll watch for Allie."

"You sure?"

"Go on."

"Mmm. Okay."

Meg couldn't fight it. She was barely aware of her arm creeping up around Nick's neck or the way her forehead rested against his chin or the easy pressure of his leg against hers. It was just exhaustion, the softness of his sweater, and slow, deep breathing.

"Meg," she heard him whisper after a while. It came from someplace far away, a place with no sharp angles or painful corners. She sighed and snuggled closer, pressing her face into the crook of his bare neck. She sensed that he was stroking her hair, but it was all so hazy that she didn't really think about it. She wanted to stay there, just like that, forever.

"Meg," Nick said again.

She turned to face him. Both her hands were against his chest and his mouth was so close to hers. She felt as if she was floating on a peaceful, warm breeze. "Hmmm?"

His eyes took in her whole face. He suddenly pulled her to him, hugging her as tightly as he could, as if he could take his burst of energy and give her half of it. Meg gave herself over to the luscious warmth, the feeling of skin and denim and wool. But then she felt herself leaning into a soft kiss, and her mind cleared up, shaking her awake. This was Nick she was with. Nick! All that was over. At least she'd told herself it was. No, it was. It had to be. She couldn't face another year of high school where everything was clouded

159

by being in love with him. She tried to stand up, furiously batting dirt and leaves off her clothes.

Nick pulled her back down. He held her hands so hard it hurt. "Meg, I broke up with Darcy."

She wasn't sure why he was telling her or how to react. "So?"

"I just wanted you to know."

"Why? When?"

"Just now. Before I left school." He shook his head. "I'm not quite sure what I ever saw in her in the first place."

Meg's head was starting to rush. Suddenly it was clear to her. Nick had just broken up with Darcy, so now he was looking for the next in his long line of adoring girl friends. She angrily wrenched her hands away and stood up. "We'd better get back."

"Meg, wait," he pleaded. "I know this sounds crazy, but sometimes I think it's you that I really care about. I know that sounds nuts."

Meg pulled her hands away and stood up. Reality was hitting her like a bucket of ice water. She could stand just being Nick's friend. But the one thing she couldn't handle was being another in his string of meaningless girl friends. She could just hear him in another month, whispering to some new girl about how he wasn't sure what he'd ever seen in Meg McCall.

"It is nuts," Meg responded harshly. She started back toward the trail, her legs suddenly burning with energy. She was getting this restless, crazy feeling now, as if she might never fall asleep again.

"Why?" Nick pleaded. "I know this is a surprise and all, but it's kind of like it's always been there. I don't know."

Meg walked faster, trying to get far enough ahead of Nick so that he couldn't touch her again. What could she say? *It's not that I don't love you, it's that I love you too much. This is easy for you. I won't mean any more to you than all the other girls you've collected junior year. But I have a lot more at stake. I'd rather not be friends at all than be the latest addition to your lengthy list.*

"Is it Patrick? Is that it?" Nick said, rushing up alongside her.

"Yes," Meg heard herself say. She pictured Patrick, his long hair and sensitive face. Maybe she didn't feel about Patrick the way she felt about Nick, but Patrick was a terrific person, thoughtful and generous and kind. She decided right there that she would throw herself into the relationship with Patrick. It was the only hope she had to get Nick out of her system once and for all. "Yes, it's Patrick."

Nick's liveliness dimmed and he slowed to a walk. "Oh. I see."

"Patrick's a great guy."

"He is."

"He likes me a lot."

"I know."

"So, that's the way it is."

Nick fell behind her. He no longer struggled to keep up. "I understand."

By the time they got back and found Celia in the driveway waving and screaming that Sean had

161

found Allie and was bringing her home, Meg was jogging and Nick was dragging himself in behind her. When they passed the tree house they were yards apart. They didn't look at one another. They didn't talk. No one would ever have known that anything had happened between them.

CHAPTER
15

Allie sat safely between Brooke and Sean in the front seat of Sean's van. A call-in talk show was on low and the engine made a steady rumble. The three of them were quiet. They passed Marin. Vacaville. Napa. It grew darker and darker until there was nothing left but the highway signs and the gray ribbon of freeway.

But the inside of Allie's head was filled with harsh color and noise. "I don't care" rang out, over and over. She kept seeing the boy on Geary Street, that strange red ponytail, the white chest, the empty, bloodshot eyes. She kept hearing his crazy laugh and smelling his leather jacket. She pictured Jack's apartment — a crash pad strewn with fast-food wrappers and old blankets. She thought about Jack. Who was he? Why did he let girls stay in his apartment? What happened to the girls who did?

Allie shivered, even though the heat was practically burning her ankles and her toes. She'd seen a mirror of her own emptiness and it terrified her. She'd also seen that there was something uglier and more hopeless than her own misery and Redwood High.

What was she supposed to do now, though? She couldn't go back to her old friends. Maybe Sean and Brooke but not the rest of them and their group. The only thing she knew was that she didn't want to give up, or be alone. She didn't want to be the one to yell "I don't care" to a stranger in the middle of San Francisco.

The Redwood Hills off-ramp came into view, and Allie heard the click, click, click of the turn signal. Brooke straightened up. Sean turned off the radio.

"Allie, what do you think your parents will do?" he asked her, breaking the long silence.

"I don't know. I just talked to my mom. When I finally called, my dad still wasn't home. Mom actually didn't get as mad as I thought she would. I guess she hadn't started to worry yet. She said we'll talk when I get home."

"Allie," Brooke said in a thoughtful voice.

"Hmm?"

"Did you know that your name is on the callback list for the play? For *Our Town*."

Allie leaned forward on the dash. They'd just turned off the freeway and were passing fields and tall trees lit only by moonlight. It seemed like ages since she left Redwood Hills that morning. And it seemed even longer since she'd gone to that audition and seen L.P. "Really? Ms. Smith really put my name down to audition again?"

"Yeah."

"Does that mean she liked me?"

"No, Al," Sean cracked. "She wants you to audition again because she thought you stunk up the joint."

Allie actually laughed, a short, low, giggle. She bumped Sean with her shoulder.

Brooke shrugged. "You don't have to go if you don't want to, but the call-backs are at lunch on Monday. I wanted to make sure you knew."

"Okay."

They grew silent again as Sean drove past Redwood High. They headed away from downtown and toward the vineyards and the ranches. The streets got darker. Soon there was the crackle of dirt road under the tires. They passed Nick's front yard and slowly approached Allie's house.

As Sean eased up the driveway he saw them in his rearview mirror. He didn't know how they'd spotted the van. There were no lights out here and Nick's house was set back from the street. Sure, Sean had called and told them about when they'd be home. But he was hoping he'd be able to quietly drop Allie off and have some time when he could at least try to patch things up with Brooke. But no. As soon as Sean put on the brake, they came racing across the apple orchard and toward the van. Celia, Meg, and Nick.

Allie tensed when she recognized them. Celia came first, her coat flapping. Meg and Nick were a few strides behind, on either side of Celia, but not close to one another.

"You know," Allie said, "I think I'd rather

165

face my parents right now, than face the three of them."

Sean turned off the engine. "Maybe it's better to take the worst first. Then your parents won't seem so bad."

Allie patted his hand. "Thanks. Both of you. I called Celia first because I was so panicked. But I'm really glad it was the two of you who came to get me instead."

Sean glanced out the window. The trio was getting closer. "Sure. Maybe it makes up for how weird I was to you when you first got back. I don't think I was a very loyal friend for a while."

Allie held his wrist. "You were better than that," she sighed. "You left me alone." Brooke opened the door and hopped down to let Allie out. Once Allie's feet touched the ground, she gave Brooke a quick hug. "Thank you."

The porch light flickered on, and Allie's father appeared at the front door. When he saw Meg, Nick, and Celia arrive at the van, he didn't go any farther, but stayed in the doorway waiting for Allie to come in.

Allie stood with Brooke while her three friends caught their breath.

"Are you okay?" Meg panted.

"What happened? We were so worried about you," Nick said.

Allie met Celia's eye. Celia looked from Allie to Brooke and back again.

Allie stopped Celia before she could say anything. "I'm sorry, Cici," Allie said. "I'm not who you want me to be and I probably never will be."

She took in Meg and Nick, too. "All I know now is what I'm not, and I have to figure what I am. And I think I'm going to have to do it away from you guys."

Before Celia could respond, Allie patted Brooke one more time and hurried into the house. They all watched as Mr. Simon held the door open. Mrs. Simon appeared briefly in the doorway, too, and then it closed.

"This is just great," Celia swore, shaking her head and glaring at Brooke.

"What?" Brooke asked.

"Here you are again. Why is it, every time Allie gets in trouble, you're there, too?"

Sean slid across the seat and jumped out, landing between Celia and Brooke. He was too angry — at Celia and himself — to sit and listen to this again. "Did you ever think that maybe you were there, too, whenever Allie got in trouble?"

"What?" Celia gasped.

"Or all of us? Or just Allie herself?"

"I happen to have a responsibility," Celia insisted. "We all do. We have to stick together, through everything. We can't give up on each other the first time one of us has a problem."

Sean threw his head back. "Celia, you have it all wrong. We grew up together. We're juniors now! We don't owe each other anything anymore, except maybe to stay out of each other's way so we can all be who we are and not part of some weird group that has to be a certain way because that's how Celia Cavenaugh sees herself!"

Celia stepped back, stunned. Meg and Nick looked at one another, then turned away.

"Is that what you really think?" Celia said in a weak voice.

Sean noticed that Brooke had taken a step closer to him. "Yes."

Celia stared at the ground. Nick and Meg had moved off even farther and the three of them seemed uncomfortable together, as if they were strangers rather than old, old friends.

"I was only doing what I thought was best," Celia said. All the punch had gone out of her voice. "For all of us."

"You probably were."

Celia's shoulders slumped forward. Meg and Nick looked wrung out and weary, but suddenly Celia looked even wearier. "I didn't mean for it to turn out like this. I'm sorry."

"Me, too," said Sean. "Come on, Brooke." He held out his hand. Brooke took it. "Let's go."

They both got back into the van and Sean started it up. He waved once as he pulled out. Celia, Nick, and Meg stood there watching, making three long, sad, separate shadows.

On the way home, Brooke slid closer to him. By the time he pulled over across the street from her house, their arms and knees were touching. He lightly tapped her foot with his.

They both looked straight ahead, staring at the huge tree sagging down over the windshield. "What a day," Sean sighed.

"Yeah."

"Do you think Allie will be okay?"

"I don't know."

He turned to her. "Brooke, I'm sorry about last weekend. I know I acted like a jerk and — "

She interrupted him by lacing her arm in his and resting her head on his shoulder. "You don't have to apologize anymore."

"I don't?"

"Nope."

"I thought you were never going to speak to me again."

She smiled. "I changed my mind."

Sean settled back into the seat, nestling against her. He smelled her baby powder again and took a deep, deep breath, savoring it and thinking how lucky he was to be there at that moment, with her.

"You know it doesn't have to be me or them," Brooke said.

"What?"

"Me or your old friends. You can still be close to them and be with me, too."

"Maybe. After a while. I'm not sure."

She was gazing at him. The streetlight trickled in through the window, just illuminating her bright eyes and a few short curls. She touched his face.

Sean caught her hand. "All I know now is that I'm crazy about you. That's sort of the highest priority on my list right now. If you know what I mean."

"Your highest priority?" Brooke laughed suddenly. "What am I, some new science experiment?"

"Hey, don't look at me. I'm not the one who attaches a clock to a potato."

"You just sing to yourself in the back of the cafeteria."

Now Sean was laughing, too. "Oh, yeah. Well,

169

you forget that you're supposed to wear two shoes."

"At least I don't dance like I have two left feet."

"Wait a minute. Are you saying I'm a bad dancer? I happen to be a very good dancer. I can do a perfect Michael Jackson spin."

"I'd love to see that."

"You would?"

She wound her arms around him and grinned. "Sure."

"Oh, Brooke," Sean sighed, wrapping his arms around her and holding on tight. "Anytime. Anytime."

CHAPTER 16

By lunchtime on Monday, Allie was so hungry she could barely stand it. Lately she hadn't been interested in food, but over the weekend her appetite had come back. Just like a little of her courage had come back and a little hope. She'd decided that she was going to the call-back audition. Even if she blew it again, even if she was a total disaster, at least she cared enough to try. That was what mattered.

She ran to the cafeteria as soon as her fourth-period class got out to grab some lunch before heading over to the drama studio. By the time she'd wolfed down her sandwich, the cafeteria was starting to fill up and get noisy. Allie hesitated on her way out, trying to remember which direction the drama studio was from there. Stalling in the doorway, she noticed something odd.

Since their first day as freshmen, she, Meg, Nick, Sean, and Celia had always eaten at the same table. It was a big round one, right in the middle of the caf. Even though Allie had avoided that table since she'd been back, she'd noticed that her friends still sat there. Actually, that table was now the social center of the lunchroom.

But today Celia was the only one. She was with Maria Martinez and Sam Pond, Jason Sandy and Jim Burke, and the rest of the popular crowd. Meg was clear over in the corner, at a small table with Patrick Delancie. Just the two of them. He gazed at her adoringly as they chatted and shared their lunches. And Nick sat near the deli counter, surrounded by a bunch of boys — jocks and a few guys from the newspaper. They were all looking over Nick's article in the new edition of *The Guardian*. Sean wasn't in the cafeteria at all.

For a moment Allie watched Meg, Nick, and Celia. They didn't seem to notice one another. They were each so involved in what he or she was doing; Meg with Patrick, Nick with his article, Celia with her crowd. Allie finally turned and went her own way.

She walked quickly, clearing thoughts of her old friends from her brain and trying to concentrate on *Our Town*. She'd checked the play out from the library over the weekend and read it twice. She'd even brought her library copy with her and looked through it during each class that morning.

She strode across the quad, past the rose bushes and the greenhouse until she came to the art rooms and the drama studio. When she got up close she saw the call-back list tacked up on the door. Amazingly, her name was really there.

There was also a note asking to open the door quietly and Allie did just that. The first thing she saw inside was Sean, sitting on the floor in the foyer eating his lunch and reading a science fiction paperback. When he saw her he raised a finger to his lips. She could hear a boy auditioning inside. She tiptoed in.

"Sean, what are you doing here?" she whispered.

He put down his book and grinned. "Waiting for Brooke."

She started to go but Sean playfully grabbed her ankle.

He looked up at her. "Good luck. I mean, break an arm. Or beam me up, or whatever I'm supposed to say."

Allie patted the top of Sean's head and tried not to laugh. "Thanks." She walked softly around the corner and slipped into a seat in the back row.

As soon as the boy onstage finished reading, Brooke turned back. She was holding a clipboard and had a hammer hanging from the loop of her overalls. She gave a tiny wave and held up crossed fingers.

Allie thumbed through her library script while two more boys read. Then her own name was called. She hadn't expected to be called so soon, and as she walked down to the stage she felt the familiar buzz of fear. Carefully, she climbed onto the stage.

"Hi, Allie," Ms. Smith said, leaning forward on the seat in front of her. "I wasn't sure you'd come."

Allie thought about the last time she tried this and the buzz turned into roar. She hoped Ms. Smith didn't think she was a mental case. She hoped the teacher hadn't made a mistake when she called her back. "I almost didn't," Allie admitted softly. "It was dumb to run out like that."

The teacher didn't take her eyes off her. "Why did you? Come back, that is."

Allie looked out at the rows of seats. All the other kids who were there to audition watched her very intently. "I wanted to come back. To give it another try."

She thought Ms. Smith was going to ask her more questions about that first audition, but Allie's answer seemed to have satisfied her. Instead the teacher asked, "What part of the play would you like to read for me?"

That took Allie by surprise. She realized that she was clutching her library copy and held it up, a little confused.

"If you want I'll assign you a page," Ms. Smith offered. "I just thought there might be a certain scene that appealed to you."

"There is," Allie heard herself say. "The part at the end where Emily comes back."

"Good. Read that. I'll read Mrs. Webb. Start whenever you're ready."

Allie'd looked over that part so often her book fell open to the exact page. It was where Emily came back from the grave and noticed all the things she hadn't appreciated when she was alive.

Allie read slowly, steadily. As she spoke, her imagination started to fill with what she was reading. Soon she could see it. Grover's Corners, the town where Emily lived. Her mother's kitchen. The tablecloth and the curtains and the sunflowers outside the window. She could smell the coffee and bacon, hear the voices of George Gibbs and Mrs. Soames. It was almost as if Emily's life was filling her instead of her own, and as Emily was saying good-bye to the world, she felt her own insides come back to life.

Then it was over. Emily had no more to say, so Allie lowered her head. That was when she felt the tears on her cheeks. She lifted her eyes. Everyone was staring at her. This time there was more than curiosity on their faces. There was sadness and pleasure and true interest.

"Thank you, Allie," Ms. Smith told her after a pause. "I'll post the results today after school. That was really lovely."

Allie mumbled a thank you of her own, and clutching her script, she climbed down off the stage and sat in the back until the entire lunch period was over.

Last class was Spanish. It was in the clump of classrooms just beyond the art rooms and the drama studio. As the final bell rang, Allie found herself wishing that she had to cross the entire campus to check the cast list. It was too easy this way. Too close. Too scary.

She could handle it if she didn't make the play, she told herself. The important thing was that she'd gone. She'd cared.

Still Allie dawdled. She went to the bathroom. She sat on the steps. She looked up and down the hallways, opened her locker, took a drink of water. Finally she headed back over to the drama studio. On the way she passed Ms. Pittman's photo room. The door was open. Allie couldn't resist peeking in.

He was there. She saw him right away. L.P. The long frame, lean face, the big canvas bag next to him with photos and boxes of film spilling out. He was bent over a table, cutting a piece of mattboard with an X-acto knife. He was concentrating so hard that he didn't hear her at all when she walked in.

"Hi," she said.

He jumped and his knife bit into his thumb. "Ouch." He brought his thumb to his mouth and blew on it. That was when he recognized her. He had on his old wire-rimmed glasses and pulled them off as if he wasn't sure he was seeing correctly. He blew on his thumb again. "Hi."

"I was passing by and I thought you might be in here."

He went back to work. "I'm in here most every day."

"You always were."

Finally L.P. stopped and looked up. "You okay?" he asked after a moment.

"I'm getting there." She started to go, then reconsidered. "L.P."

"Yes, Al?"

"When I told you not to come to New York, to see me. . . ." Allie lost her nerve.

"Yes."

"I guess I wanted you to know, it didn't have anything to do with you. It was me. I was in bad shape, and I didn't want anyone to see me. Especially you."

"Why especially me?"

"Because I cared about you most of all."

He took a step toward her.

"Does that make sense, L.P.?"

"A little."

"I'm sorry I hurt you."

L.P. came very close. Gently, he smoothed a strand of hair away from her eyes.

Just then the red warning light over the darkroom went out and the door swung open. The girl who'd been with L.P. the day of the first audition walked out, blinking from the bright light. She was blonde and soft-looking, probably a sophomore.

"Hi," she said, surprised but trying not to sound angry. She stared at Allie and L.P.

L.P. took an intentional step back. "Betsy, this is Allie." He held his hand out to Betsy.

Betsy came over and stood next to him. "Hi, Allie."

Allie nodded.

Betsy looked up at L.P., then offered a tentative smile to Allie. "I'm sorry I used that flash in the drama studio that day. It was a really stupid thing to do."

"That's okay."

"L.P.'s told me a lot about you."

Allie backed up toward the door. She didn't run or bolt or feel like crying. She just wanted to get going, to get on with her life. She stopped in the doorway and said, "Nice to meet you, Betsy. Maybe we'll see each other around school."

"I hope so," said L.P.

" 'Bye."

" 'Bye, Al."

Allie raised one hand and, without looking back, walked out.

She continued slowly to the drama studio. She'd known before that Betsy was L.P.'s new girl friend, so she wasn't shocked. Oddly enough, she felt calmer, more free. It was officially over. For her and for L.P.

Now she walked eagerly toward the drama studio, unable to think about anything but the audition and the play that would happen in the future. Soon she saw the door and the list and two girls standing in front of it. As she approached they both passed by her and smiled.

Allie held her breath until she looked at it. Then she stood there for a long time, just taking it in. It was there in black and white. Allie Simon hadn't screwed up this time. She had been cast as Emily in the Redwood High production of *Our Town.*

There was a loud knock on the screen door.

"Great," Nick cursed, startled and annoyed at the interruption. Of course, he could hardly expect Celia and his aunt to stay away so he could use their living room as an office. He trudged across the shag carpet and wondered why he hadn't heard the car pull up or seen the headlights through the drapes. He opened the door.

It wasn't Celia. Or her mother. It was Meg.

"Hi."

"Oh. Hi."

Her hair was pulled back in a sloppy ponytail, but she was holding a fancy dress, covered in plastic, against her torso. She made Nick think of those cut-out cardboard statues at amusement parks where you took a picture of somebody's face over the body of Snow White or Cinderella.

Meg stepped back when he pushed the screen door open. Her dress rustled and crunched. He stared into her blue eyes for what seemed like ages. How long had it been since he and Meg were together, alone? he found himself wondering. How long?

Meg didn't say a word. She just stared back and clutched her dress more tightly.

"Hi," Nick whispered again, finally.

"Is Celia here?"

"Celia?" His brain had gone blank. All he could take in was Meg's eyes and her mouth and the wisps of dark hair streaming down the sides of her face.

She tried to look past him, but he sensed that it was only an excuse not to meet his gaze. "I wanted to show her my dress. For the prom."

"She's not home."

"What are you doing here?"

Nick hesitated. He wasn't sure how much to say. "My room's being painted at home," he heard himself lie. "So I came here instead."

Meg didn't look convinced. Still, she didn't pursue it. "Do you know when Cici's getting back?"

It was as if they were total strangers, not two people who'd spent half their lives together, practically thinking as one. "No. I just got here and let myself in."

Meg backed up. More rustling and crunching. "Well. I guess, oh, tell her to call me. She wanted me to see her prom dress, too." Nick was leaning out, still holding the screen door open. She had backed all the way to the edge of the Astroturf. "Okay?"

"Okay."

She stopped. "I'll be at home." She gestured to her house next door, as if he didn't know where she lived.

Nick could see her parents through the kitchen window, past the potted plants and the porch swing. They were doing the dishes and laughing. That was when Nick flashed back to the last time he and Meg were really alone together. Over a year ago. In the woods behind his house. They were looking for Allie. Meg fell asleep in his arms, and he'd watched her sleeping and thought how he'd never loved anybody as much as he loved her. He suddenly looked away, afraid that his thoughts were going to burst out, and Meg would read them all over his face.

She was still standing on the walkway. She hadn't budged. "Nick, are you okay?"

"Sure." Nick forced himself to smile. "If you want, you can come in and wait. I'm sure Celia will be home soon. She's got to be off work by now."

"I don't want to interrupt you or anything."

"It's okay."

"Are you sure?"

"It's fine."

"Honest?"

Nick swallowed hard. "Honest."

"Okay. I guess." When she entered the house they each did an awkward little dance to get out of the other's way. Meg carefully laid her dress over the TV. She started to sit on the sofa, but when Nick sat there, she moved to the easy chair instead.

"So that's your prom dress?"

"Uh-huh. Do you think it's okay?"

Nick shrugged. The way it was slung over the TV it just looked like a sheet of plastic-covered blue. "I'm sure Patrick'll like it."

"Are you going?" Meg seemed nervous, crossing and recrossing her legs. She was wearing running shorts and an old sweat shirt. Her feet were bare. "What a dumb question. Of course you're going. You're nominated for prom king."

"I bought a ticket." Nick suddenly got the feeling that she wanted to know who he was going with. He hadn't asked anybody. There was no one he wanted to ask. "I guess I'd better hurry up and find a date. Got any suggestions?" He laughed.

"I'm sure there are plenty of girls who'd give anything to go with you."

"Yeah? Name twelve." She laughed, too. After the laugh ended, it got so quiet that Nick could hear the crickets again. He picked up his notepad and started to doodle. "Sean told me you got accepted premed at Berkeley." She nodded. "Congrats. That's great. I'm going there, too. Journalism major."

"I know. Celia told me."

"Yeah? It's a huge school, but who knows, maybe we'll see each other."

"Maybe."

It's a Night to Remember...

Last Dance

Sequel to Saturday Night!

by Caroline B. Cooney

Happiness and heartbreak are in the air. Eight months have passed since that special, memorable Autumn Leaves Dance. Now it's June, time for the last dance of the school year. Anne, wiser and more beautiful than ever, just wants to survive it. Beth Rose is more in love than ever...but wants Gary to fall in love with her, too. Emily, her safe world suddenly shattered, turns to Matt to make it right. Molly has been rejected, and she's out for revenge. Kip has been having the time of her life, and hopes the dance will be the perfect ending to the school year.

It will be romantic for some, heartbreaking for others...but above all, a dance the girls will never forget!

Look for it wherever you buy books!

$2.50 U.S./$3.95 CAN

Scholastic Books

LD871

Don't miss the...

It is the best of times. It is the worst of times. It is a time of wishes, hopes, hurts, fears, and loves. It's high school ...and they're the Class of '88.

Nick the golden boy, Celia the beautiful, Sean the thinker, Allie the wild, and Meg the brave. They have been friends since grade school. They've played and worked together, grown up, supported, even loved each other for years. Will high school tear them apart? Find out!

Read them all!

☐ 40348-6

FRESHMAN

☐ 40349-4

SOPHOMORE

☐ 40350-8

☐ 40351-6

$2.50 each.

Available wherever you buy books...or use the coupon below.